PACK YOUR BAGS, MAGGIE DIAZ

PACK YOUR BAGS, MAGGIE DIAZ

Written by **NINA MORENO**
Illustrated by **COURTNEY LOVETT** and **ASIA SIMONE**

SCHOLASTIC PRESS / NEW YORK

Library of Congress Cataloguing-in-Publication Data available

ISBN 978-1-338-81861-1

10 9 8 7 6 5 4 3 2 1   23 24 25 26 27

Printed in Italy   183

First edition, May 2023
Book design by Maeve Norton

For Florida kids,

My fellow moody, eerie, thoughtful,
radical, powerful Florida kids.

✳ CHAPTER 1 ✳

After being majorly stressed out for the first half of the school year, I realized that seventh grade is a piece of cake. Sure, I had to get grounded, almost fail math, and try out a bunch of different clubs, but it all worked out perfectly.

Just like I planned.

MAGGIE'S To-Do List
☑ JOIN A CLUB
☑ MAKE THE HONOR ROLL
☑ GET A PHONE
☑ GET PERMISSION TO RIDE MY BIKE TO THE PARK

MISSION ACCOMPLISHED!

Now I've got a phone and I'm no longer sharing my bedroom with my abuela and her stash of vitamins. I'm even allowed to hang out at the beach with my best friends, Zoey and Julian, *without* parental supervision (though my mom still watches my GPS location like a hawk).

My independence is all thanks to the golden ticket of my latest very shiny report card.

I recommend that anyone trying to get out from under their parents' thumb make honor roll, if they can swing it. It worked like a charm for my sometimes strict but usually okay Cuban American parents.

"Magdalena! Get in here right now!"

Well . . . it mostly worked.

I slide into the kitchen in socked feet while wearing a mostly clean school uniform and find the kitchen in its usual weekday-morning chaotic state.

My baby brother, Lucas, is in his high chair at the table making an epic mess of his morning oatmeal. Dad is attempting to fry a bunch of bacon with only his left hand since his right arm is now in a sling thanks to a recent injury at work. Caro is working on some school assignment at the table. Now that it's her second semester of eleventh grade, the only thing my annoyingly perfect older sister can talk about is applying to college. And

that's only when she isn't going all intense drill sergeant on me as she "helps" me practice for next week's track-and-field tryouts.

Abuela is pouring a round of Cuban coffee while listening to the radio report local news in rapid-fire Spanish. Mom is frantically searching the cabinets above the sink.

"I cannot find a single cup. Why can I not find a single cup in this house?" She spins toward me. Her hair's a little frazzled—almost as bad as my own morning bedhead. "How many dirty cups are in your room right now, Magdalena?"

That's two times she's full-named me in less than two minutes. Not a good sign at any point, but especially bad on a frantic Monday morning. I hated it when Abuela moved in with us last summer and took over half my room and one of my bunk beds with all her minty medicine and old lady knickknacks. It was an invasion of privacy and major loss of independence.

But I'd never been so tidy.

Now that she is living in the tiny house Dad built for her in our backyard, my personal habitat is back to its natural, messy state.

My report card is the shiniest thing about me these days, but that's okay. It's what Mom would call work-life balance. If she wasn't mad about the three cups with varying levels of water currently in my room.

"I'll wash every single one of them," I promise Mom.

"Maggie," she whines as she continues her search for some kind of glassware or mug, but at least we're back to Maggie instead of Magdalena.

My phone buzzes in my pocket. I grin as I take it out and check the screen. I've had it for two months now, but I still get excited whenever I get a text.

Mom's still on the hunt for a cup, but she doesn't bother to open and look

in our dishwasher, because for whatever reason, my family doesn't use ours. It's a place to store pots, pans, and all the plastic containers Abuela

refuses to throw out and instead hand-washes before reusing.

Thankfully, she gives up the search and focuses on her tiny cup of strong Cuban coffee instead.

Mom's a little tense seeing as how it's her first day at her new job as an official accountant. She finished her degree in December and is going from the frying pan to the fire (as Dad jokes *again* before *definitely* burning the bacon, as evident by the rank smell in here) because it's tax season. I've never heard of this season. As a kid from Florida, the only seasons I know about are summer, summer junior, that one intense cold front we get in January, and hurricane season.

I grab a slice of pan tostado and am about to add an extra dollop of butter when Caro suddenly shouts, "I am *so* over polynomial equations!" and startles all of us in the kitchen.

Seventh grade put a lot of pressure on me to figure out who I am. But according to Caro, it's even worse in eleventh grade, because everyone wants to know who you're going to become next.

"¿Polynomial . . . qué? Qué es eso?" Abuela asks. She's wearing teal leggings and a very flashy and bright

windbreaker jacket. Inspired by my journey through clubs and activities last semester, Abuela is now tackling several different hobbies and sports, in search of her own self-discovery. And she's wrangling every retired old person she knows along the way.

Who am I to talk her out of it? My school club–hopping quest totally worked out. My grades have never been better, and it turns out that I actually do like running. Plus, I'm hanging out with my best friends all the time. My best friend Zoey is a killer flutist in band, and my other best friend, Julian, is an amazing artist who even got to design and paint a city mural across from my favorite bakery.

We've all figured out our extracurricular skills and now that we're past winter break, my next big plan is to officially make the track team, keep my grades up to continue impressing my parents, have fun with Julian and Zoey, and have the *best* spring break field trip ever with my friends.

The seventh-grade spring break trip is a huge deal. It's four days and will be my first time going anywhere without my parents. I'm daydreaming about possible locations when Mom shrieks, *"My blouse!"*

I nearly spill my juice as Dad yelps at the stove over the sound of angry bacon hissing and spitting oil.

Mom snatches up a paper towel, grabbing way too many in her panic. The roll starts to rapidly unfurl behind her before Abuela jumps forward and tears the sheets off. Mom doesn't even notice as she quickly blots at the brand-new coffee stain spreading across her shirt.

"I'm going to be late now!" Mom races down the hall toward her room in total meltdown mode.

Dad switches off the stove and comes over to Caro and me. He quietly but seriously says, "I need advice."

"Stop trying to cook bacon with only your left hand," I tell him.

"It's about Valentine's Day. Your mom has been so stressed, I want to make sure I get her something really good this year," he says with a big cheesy smile.

"Gross," I say around a bite of toast.

"¡Qué romántico!" Abuela sings.

"That's sweet, Dad." Caro stops packing up her homework to smile at him. It's that lovesick smile of hers. Now that she officially has a girlfriend cooler than her, she's been all moony-eyed and listening to crybaby acoustic songs in her room all night. "Alex is taking me to an escape room."

Dad looks impressed. "Fun!"

"Probably to escape *you*," I tease.

Abuela takes the opportunity to tell us all about a recent episode of her current favorite telenovela where some dude took his lady love out on a moonlit horseback ride by the ocean.

"By moonlight? Sounds dangerous," I say.

"No, it sounds romantic," Caro argues wistfully.

Dad looks thoughtful, like he's taking a mental note.

It's official. Love is in the air at the Diaz house. I grab my backpack and race right out of there before I get infected, too.

★ CHAPTER 2 ★

Something else this formerly C-average student did not know before leveling up last semester is that there are

many elite privileges that come with making the honor roll. That little certificate really opens up a whole new world to a seventh grader.

It's not easy living the high life, but I'm happy to do it.

Okay, so I didn't *really* get any of that (not even the perfect pancake ... tragic) but I made a plan and it *worked*.

I'm pretty sure I'm a magician or something. Or maybe I take after my abuela more than I thought and I'm a fellow bruja in the making.

I park my bike in my regular crowded spot and then head to breakfast with Zoey and Julian. I quickly scarf down some French toast sticks while Julian tells us all about the latest sketches for his comic and Zoey updates us on her little sister's insistence that she's actually a cat now. To her Haitian American parents' total confusion, their youngest has been demanding to wear a fuzzy orange tail with her school uniform. According to Zoey, her little sister is wearing down her parents *and* the elementary school.

I can't help but be impressed. "Like I've said," I tell them, "a good plan always works."

"You're not the one who has to deal with a sister who won't stop meowing," Zoey grumbles.

"No, mine is just in *love*." I complain about Caro's moody midnight playlists. "She even called the radio and made a dedication."

This next one goes out to Alex.

Zoey laughs, but Julian calls it sweet.

I roll my eyes. "She's a total simp."

"Look around," Julian says. "Everyone is lately."

To my horror, I notice that he's right. As we head down the half before first bell, I see red-and-pink heart posters and decorations on the walls among all the announcements, club sign-up sheets, and inspirational posters. One in particular catches my eye.

I spin toward Zoey and Julian. "Where do you think we'll get to go?" When Caro was in seventh grade, her class got to go to *Orlando*. I'd love to go to some theme parks with my friends.

"Hopefully not the Everglades," Zoey says.

"Nothing with heights." Julian shudders. "And not Jungle Island again."

"And nothing with airboats!"

We split at our usual spot since Zoey and Julian both have Mr. Jones for homeroom, while I'm stuck in Mrs. Delgado's room. When I

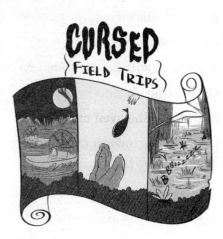

pass the woodshop, Mr. Santiago sticks his head out and smiles. "Ms. Diaz! Guess what the eighth graders are

building this week?"

I breathlessly* ask, "Skateboards?"

He laughs. "Be sure to sign up again when track and field is over."

Woodworking was one of my favorite clubs last semester, and even though it turned out that it wasn't my calling, I still had a lot of fun. But after doing cross-country, I can't wait for the relays, hurdles, maybe even some high jumps. The only downside to trying out for the track team is that running has also *always* been Caro's thing. And her name is still *all* over the trophies outside our school gym.

Soon it will be *my* name on those awards.

First bell rings and everyone scatters toward homeroom. I hurry to mine, duck into the

room, and jump over Eddie's backpack where he always leaves it in the aisle between our desks.

"Hey, Moody Maggie," he says without turning around.

"Hey yourself, Eerie Eddie." We both laugh as I settle into my seat.

Another upside to having tried out so many clubs is that way more people know my name these days.

It's really nice to not have everyone referring to me as Caro's little sister anymore.

My academic upswing is all thanks to tutoring twice a week after school and excellent organizational skills when it comes to my notes and disastrous binder.

It's all for the greater good, even though I'm pretty sure that the back pain from carrying all this stuff around will outlast anything I learn in algebra.

Not to mention that my English teacher is making us write *way* too many essays this semester. Talking about anything for five paragraphs is torture, let alone writing a compelling narrative essay about being the new kid in school when I've never even moved to a different city. My introductory paragraphs are never any match for my wandering thoughts and repetitive sentences.

Enough to say, it's a relief to make it to lunch.

As great as lunch is, the cafeteria can be a lonely place, so I'm super grateful for the certainty of our table again. Not only have I learned time management and study skills, I also don't get all in my head or insecure about my friends anymore. I never want to fight with either of them again. And we won't because we *communicate* now.

Like I said, I've totally leveled up.

Zoey stops to chat with Maya and some of her other band friends before coming to sit beside me, and I wave at

Eerie Eddie, who still likes to sit alone. He gave me refuge last semester and even shared his quesadilla once. Julian brings over his wild pack of art kids before they leave to get in line.

Julian digs into his food with fewer table manners than usual. He has four older teenage brothers and says that if he doesn't eat fast enough, he doesn't eat at all. But this is messy even for him.

"Sometimes I forget that you're a boy." Zoey pushes her own lunch aside and pulls a book out of her bag.

"Sorry," he says around a huge bite. "I can't be late for the new student orientation."

I frown, confused. "You're not a new student."

He pushes his now-empty tray toward Zoey's abandoned one. "I volunteered to give the new kid a tour."

"Really?" I ask. "Why?"

"Out of the goodness of my heart."

Zoey looks up from her book wearing the same confused expression as me. Julian laughs. Aside from us and the art kids, he's not super social or all that interested in extracurriculars.

"Ms. Pérez offered my name to the guidance counselor because the new kid is joining art club. Plus, it's getting me out of health class."

"Nice!" I say. I did some volunteering with the Future Leaders club and it was pretty cool. Getting approval to leave class was always a thrill. I'd never felt so important or more part of the school.

But between track and tutoring, I don't

have time to be in all those clubs again. Still, though, I'd do just about anything to get out of health class. We already talked about our changing bodies in fifth grade, but we're back to it again.

Julian dashes off toward the front office, leaving me and Zoey alone for the last ten minutes of lunch. I plan on letting her read. Honestly, I do. She's mentioned before how annoying it is that other kids don't always respect the sanctity of silent reading.

But I cave after thirty seconds. "Where do you think the field trip will be to?"

Zoey turns a page. "I have no idea."

"Let's brainstorm!" I grab a pen and my napkin. "Maybe somewhere on the west coast of Florida this time." I write that down. "They've got cool beaches, I guess. But what's in Tampa? Do they have sharks? My mom says everyone's got sharks now."

"I have to finish this before the end of the day so I can get my extra credit report done."

If honor roll students really did get perks, Zoey would be queen. Nothing—and I mean nothing—has ever threatened her straight-A streak.

"It's cool," I say. And it is. As much as I like talking to my friends, I've learned to be okay with the quiet. My favorite speed reader turns to the next page and I get to work scribbling down my ideas for the most perfect spring break field trip ever.

★ CHAPTER 3 ★

Monday, after school. Track-and-field tryouts, day one.

Today is the first day of tryouts. We have to meet everyone out on the field after school. Coach Schwartz said to
be there by 3:10 or ELSE. I'm guessing the ominous *or
else* simply means we won't be picked, but still. It's a little
dramatic.

I make it there by 3:07. Because I. Am. Ready.

I've been running for *weeks* now. Long distance. Sprints. In the mornings and sometimes even after dinner. My nosy old neighbors who sit out on their porch, drinking their coffee and gossiping while playing their card games and dominoes, love shouting my times out to me.

And if that wasn't enough, there's also Caro's very aggressive workout (torture) plan that she has subjected me to since December.

Coach Schwartz has nothing on my type-A sister.

The track is busy with everyone who's trying out—including all three grade levels—but as the week progresses, we'll be split up for all the different

events. There's the 800-, 400-, 200-, and 100-meter races (who knew I'd have to do math to run), along with team relays and the high and long jumps. Last semester, I really liked cross-country, but as much as I might like running . . . track and field feels *way* more complicated.

I'm relieved that today is meant for beginners. Because today is the mile run. The bread and butter of this whole adventure. Or better yet, pan tostado.

I take off. And as I get going and feel that burn in my leg muscles and lungs, my nervousness about tryouts disappears. It's just like cross-country. I smile as I pick up speed. I can do this. Seventh grade isn't even over yet, and I've already figured out my thing! My passion! I've figured out this huge part of my identity before the due date! The certainty of knowing I'm good at something is a total thrill. Just like Julian has art, and Zoey has band and her amazing grades, I have running.

And so what if my older, obnoxiously perfect sister also runs and is sort of responsible for me blazing past

all these sixth graders like a boss? That's not the point. The point is that I figured this out for myself.

I'm feeling pretty confident until they start separating us and direct us to run one by one. I liked that cross-country was about finding my pace, but here, with everyone looking, the competitiveness kicks in and I want to be really fast.

After the mile, Coach gathers us all near the bleachers. He pitches his voice loud and calls out, "Okay, great job on that jog, everyone."

Jog? Hold up. That was just a jog?

"Now let's get into some dynamic stretching!"

I'm trying to figure out the difference between dynamic

stretching and the regular kind when my worst nightmare comes true and Caro walks out onto the track. I freeze in place. Coach lets out a cheer. I muffle a whine.

Why is my *sister* here? This isn't fair! Today is about me, not my sister's looming shadow. But by the sounds of it, Coach and his assistant are ready to start a parade over her arrival. This is ridiculous!

"Carolina Diaz is an accomplished runner visiting us from the high school. She'll be helping with tryouts today and at our future practices."

My eyes widen. *Excuse me!*

"Everyone be sure to listen to her, because she knows her stuff!"

Sammy Marquez—another seventh grader who was on

the track team last year—leans close to me. "Isn't that your sister?"

Maggie, your sister is here!

It's controlled chaos as we all spread out and follow Caro's upbeat instructions. She never sounds this cheery when barking at me to pick up my feet as I race around the block. Positive reinforcement? She's never heard of it. But now all my fellow classmates are suddenly Olympic athletes as they try to impress my sister, while I'm the grumpy gremlin in the back.

I take all my frustration out during the different events. And when it's my turn to take off, I don't mind the spotlight. My drive to be the fastest is even bigger now. It's a whole monster with sharp teeth and very fast feet. Cheers go out from others as I turn the corner.

I spy Coach saying something to Caro as they both conspire against me. Or maybe they're just checking my time. Either way, I ignore the pinch in my chest and pick up my pace. When I cross the finish line, I'm breathing hard.

This is why I'm always telling you that breathing is an exercise, too.

I found something I was good at and actually liked, and my sister came along and ruined it.

That's it. She leaves me no choice.

"¡Señoritas no gritan en esta casa!" Abuela shouts from the kitchen. She stirs whatever's for dinner and the smell of roasted garlic, onion, and peppers makes my stomach grumble.

"I have a good reason for my shouting today, Abuela."

ABUELA!

I lift my backpack and binder onto the kitchen table, and they fall over with a heavy thunk. The amount of stuff I have to carry around all day is no joke. "Carolina is bossing me around at school. The *one* place I'm supposed to be free of her."

"I was not bossing you around." Caro fills a glass with water. "I was coaching you."

"You are *not* my coach." I whip open my binder and check my agenda again. I actually write down my homework now and it's helping me not forget stuff. "You are a high school student. Go back to high school."

"I'm volunteering." She shrugs. "It looks good on my college applications."

Abuela sets down her wooden spoon. "Yo también soy voluntaria!"

"Ugh, no fair! I want to hang out with dogs!" I complain.

"Well, you sure smell like one," Caro shoots back.

"*Abuela!*"

Abuela turns up the radio on an old-school salsa song.

Caro skips past me. "If you don't like it, you can quit. Unlike you, I'm going to take a shower before dinner."

I'll keep running. But not because of Caro. Because when I make the team, it will be *my* name on the trophies.

✳ CHAPTER 4 ✳

This Friday is the *best* Friday ever. And let me tell you, I love a Friday. Pizza Friday. Movie Friday. Fun Friday. But this Friday? This Friday is Amazing News Friday.

I made the track team! I mean, most people who tried out also made it as long as they had a good attitude. But still! I made the team!

And we're going to Saint Augustine for our spring break trip!

We're not just staying in south Florida to roam the Everglades. No camping in the humidity at Crystal River (I do love the manatees, though) or melting all day at Jungle Island again. Saint Augustine is historical and weird and *haunted*. And it's probably way better than Tampa.

The update spreads fast, and by lunch, the entire seventh grade is buzzing with the news.

SLAM!

"Can you believe it?" I ask, excited. "*Saint Augustine.* This is going to be amazing. I just have to get my parents to sign the permission slip, but after honor roll? Come on, I've got this."

Zoey is distracted and doing schoolwork instead of eating lunch again. I feel like Abuela when I nudge her forgotten tray closer to her.

"Aren't you excited?" I ask her.

"Sure," she says, sounding distracted. "But I won't be allowed to go if my grades sink."

"That's never going to happen," I tell her confidently. When she looks like she doesn't believe me, I laugh. "Zoey. *Miami* will sink before your grades."

"That's super depressing and also kind of sweet."

Julian drops down onto the bench beside me. "*That's* Maggie's specialty." He turns his wide eyes on me. "Did you hear?"

I grin. "I'm halfway to a full itinerary, buddy."

Julian laughs and digs right into his cheese calzone. "I don't think we're the ones who get to plan the trip."

"As a former Future Leader—"

With a mouth full of food, Julian cuts in. "You were in that club for barely a month."

"And you had to quit because you got in major trouble," Zoey adds without looking up from her huge binder.

Leave it to your friends to support you. And call you out

mid-bite and -sentence.

"It's called growth, thank you very much. Oh! And I made the track team!"

Zoey and Julian let out a cheer. Julian grabs me

by the shoulders and shakes me dramatically until I'm cracking up. My friends are the best.

Behind us, someone calls out Julian's name. His head whips around as his face breaks out into a big, goofy grin. He's oblivious to the marinara sauce all over his chin from eating so fast.

"Hey!" he says, and jumps to his feet with his empty tray. "This is Vanessa. She's new here."

It's not weird for Julian to have other friends. But never another girl. This feels . . . new.

"She's who I gave the tour to the other day."

I subtly point at my chin and he gives me a confused look for a second before understanding and hurriedly wiping away the marinara on his face. He then checks his shirt in a panic. He's usually covered in stains from his art supplies. Why does the idea of marinara on his shirt scare him?

"Do you want to sit with us?" he asks Vanessa, and it surprises me. We have other friends, but except for that awful fight with Zoey last semester, it's only ever the three of us at lunch together. The terrific trio. The three caballeros. Getting back to that routine assured me that everything was okay again and back to normal.

Vanessa sits down across from Julian, next to Zoey. Julian starts talking her ear off and it's nothing about Saint Augustine or making field trip plans for the three of us. But it's fine. We have time to coordinate everything later and I'm sure Vanessa won't sit with us every day.

Thanks to my expanded bike-riding privileges, instead of having to fly straight home from school, my parents now let me stop at my favorite bakery on the way.

These days Pablo's hair has gone from bright blue to a darker red that reminds me of guava. His family runs the market, while he's in charge of the bakery window. He's also responsible for all my favorite sugar-loaded, deliciously baked after-school snacks.

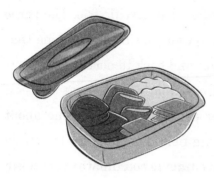

"Have you talked to your parents about—" I start to ask, but Pablo's eyes go all frantic and he quickly waves his hands to quiet me. Over his shoulder, I spot his dad. I shake my head and, sounding way older than me *or* him, I ask, "Pablo. Really?"

"I know, I know," he says, sounding tired. He drops his head as he leans his elbows against the counter. Pablo wants to bake more than just the guava pastelitos everyone in this very Cuban American neighborhood expects. He loves experimenting with all kinds of fancy desserts that he lets me taste test for him, and honestly, he's amazing. It's all fluffy pastries, creamy chocolates, and unexpected flavor combinations.

One time he even made me cookies with flowers in them! They looked weird but tasted amazing, like everything else he makes. Some fancy restaurant in town

TIRAMISU

LAYERED CAKE

CRÈME BRÛLÉE

CHEESE CAKE

offered him a job working under their baker, and Pablo is dying for the experience.

But it means telling his parents that he wants to leave this window. And turns out that no matter how old you are, telling your parents something they don't want to hear never gets any easier.

"You just have to make a plan," I tell him, and it feels repetitive, sure, but it totally works. The fact that I'm even here right now without parental supervision and my mom doesn't think I've been kidnapped or fallen into the ocean is proof of it.

Pablo smiles before offering me an extra pastelito for the road.

Much like Pablo, I have to be careful when presenting my parents (read: Mom) with any new plans or big ideas.

This trip will be my first away from home and without my family. I know that a lot of kids my age are allowed to do a *lot* more stuff than I am and hang out without their parents or family all the time. Meanwhile, I can count on

one hand how many slumber parties I've been to.

So, a sleepaway, four-day field trip is a Very Big Deal. And because conversations are *very* important in my family and my mother is a nerdy accountant who loves facts and data, I prepared an after-dinner presentation all about the upcoming field trip.

"Just imagine if you put this much effort into actual schoolwork," Caro says. "Or track."

"Not. My. Coach."

"And there will be lots of chaperones, right?" Mom asks. "Wait, why didn't I get asked to chaperone?"

"You're very busy, Mom," I say. "Tax season," I explain under my breath, because I want to keep her stress levels in check until she signs my permission slip.

"No estoy muy seguro de esto," Abuela says, and I'm shocked to my core. Ever since we were roommates, Abuela has had my back on a lot of stuff. We're supposed to be allies and so I never imagined I would have to convince her to let me go. "Esa ciudad está embrujada."

"Saint Augustine is not haunted," I argue, even though that was one of my selling points.

"It's just a few ghost tours," I say, and before Abuela can interrupt, I quickly add, "And they'll be very chaperoned and educational!"

"I've been plenty of times for work," Dad offers. He works the cranes for a salvage company and has traveled to a bunch of port cities. "Nice place."

Mom thoughtfully studies my presentation as I wait for my verdict.

Yes! I'm going to Saint Augustine!

⭐ CHAPTER 5 ⭐

Maggie: permission slip status check
Julian: 👍
Maggie: me too!!!
Maggie: Z??
Julian: 👀
Zoey: my mom wants to talk to my dad first
Maggie: no worries I KNOW they'll let you go
Zoey: hopefully
Julian: 🍀 🍀 🍀 🍀 ⛺ ⛺ ⛺

Julian will love the museums and Zoey will stop to listen to all the buskers along Saint George Street. We'll run around the hotel and stay up late. We'll take

ST AUGUSTINE
To Do:
☐ TROLLEY
☐ HAUNTED TOURS
☐ FORT
☐ CHOCOLATE TASTING
☐ ALLIGATOR FARM
☐ PIRATE MUSEUM

a million pictures and buy goofy souvenirs and it will be awesome.

At lunch on Monday, I race to the cafeteria, grab a tray, and then hurry to meet Zoey and Julian at our table. If anyone can understand having strict parents, it's me. Luckily, Ms. Pérez told me permission slips aren't due yet, so Zoey has time for her parents to warm up to the idea. Zoey's brilliant and never gets into trouble. There's no way they won't let her go. Outside, I notice that there's already three people sitting at our table. Vanessa is back.

I set my tray down. "Guess what I heard—"

"You've been to New York City?" Julian asks excitedly.

"What? No—" I start to say, confused, but realize he's talking to Vanessa.

She nods. "Yeah, with my family last summer."

"Well, it's no Saint Augustine," I joke.

"Saint Augustine is just an older Daytona Beach compared to New York City," Julian scoffs.

Even I know that New York is a big deal with more fancy stuff than anywhere in Florida, but it bothers me that Julian is so impressed by it. Especially since Saint Augustine is easily one of our top five coolest cities.

"Saint Augustine is amazing," I argue, feeling defensive.

"Have you ever been?" Vanessa asks me. And her tone *sounds* nice, but I have my suspicions.

"No . . . but it has trolleys that take you everywhere."

Julian laughs. "New York has subways."

"Since when did you become obsessed with New York?" Everyone at the table looks at me. My tone does *not* sound nice.

"Vanessa and I have to go." Julian grabs his tray and gets to his feet. I want to apologize so he'll stay, but I glance at Vanessa and feel too embarrassed. I dig into my grilled cheese.

"Where you headed?" Zoey asks them.

"We're going to stop by the library before next period. Art club project."

"See you," Vanessa says to us, and then they're gone.

"The library?" I look at Zoey. "Since when does Julian ever go to the library?"

Zoey is staring after him, a frown tugging her brows low, as she sips her water. "It does seem out of character."

1 Suspect
☐ Goes to the library
☐ Doesn't care about the trip
☐ Dresses better

I gasp as it hits me. I've seen this ailment before. "Oh *no*."

"What?" Zoey asks.

"I think Julian has a . . . crush."

Zoey gasps.

Wide-eyed, we both stare after our fallen brethren.

And then . . . suddenly I notice a definite shift in the vibes at school. As I glance around, it becomes clear that it's not just the Diaz household. Everyone around me is pairing off or crushing on someone these days.

It's not that I have anything against crushes. I'm not immune to butterflies over anime characters and even once considered buying a *Vampire Knight* poster but chickened out when Mom asked me a hundred questions about it.

But ever since winter break, it feels like everyone has been losing their minds over who is or isn't in a relationship. Like it's suddenly of dire importance. And listen, I'm not being a baby about this. Ever since the second grade, we've had classmates pretending to be in these big, great romances . . . before breaking up by the

end of the school day. It just seems ridiculous. Because even when they do finally start going out with someone, instead of being all ridiculously romantic like Caro, couples my age seem to avoid each other. I'm pretty sure I talk to Julian *way* more than some of these kids talk to their boyfriends.

A giant waste of time, if you ask me.

"Hey, can I borrow a pen?" Eddie asks, and I reach into my bag for one. When I offer it to him, his hand touches mine. My fingers tingle like when my hand falls asleep.

Huh. Weird.

At track practice after school, we run like I expect, but there are also games. Coach calls out different animals and we have to change our running tempo based on that animal's speed. We're all out of breath and laughing until we fall over.

But there's no escape from the lovesick zombies.

When we take a water break, Sammy and her best friend, Alicia, pull me in close (despite how sweaty we all are) to whisper to me about an eighth grader.

I know his name is

Josh. I go to school with a lot of Joshes, though, so I'm not sure which one he is. He's no anime character, but I guess

he's cute. He's definitely taller than the other boys. Maybe that's all it is: height. Is Vanessa tall? Am *I* tall?

When Mom picks me up from school, I ask her if Dad is taller than her.

"A little, but not by much. Why?"

"Just curious." I remember Dad asking me to do a little research for him and his big Valentine's Day plans. "So . . . what's your favorite food these days?"

"Hmm. I've been craving good ramen lately."

We have a nearby café that makes really good milk tea and the spicy ramen Mom loves.

"But our usual spot for that will be way too busy for Valentine's."

"Don't worry, I already knew," she says. "Your dad is terrible at being sneaky. Don't tell him I know."

"Okay."

"But I do not want Italian this time."

Couples are so weird.

✶ CHAPTER 6 ✶

This weekend is my first official track meet. I spend Thursday afternoon running around the neighborhood. For the first time in weeks, Caro isn't bothering me or barking out orders. I can't help but be both suspicious *and* annoyed, because as it turns out, her bossy help has been *somewhat* useful. But thanks to Valentine's Day, I get daydreaming, distracted Caro instead of aggressive-coaching Caro.

Don't ask me how, but it's worse.

"Another lap?" she asks when I keep running past our driveway.

"No, thanks!" I shout back, breathless as I spot Mrs.

García in her garden. Mrs. García lives next door and I'm pretty sure she's another neighborhood bruja. While Abuela is all about taking care of us with her vitamins, soups, and saint candles, Mrs. García has the wildest yard filled with all kinds of tropical fruits, the brightest flowers I've ever seen, and vines that grow between the trees and sometimes block out the sun. She also dresses in very shiny robes, and big, flashy gemstone rings dot all

her fingers.

"Ven acá," she calls out to me, summoning me closer even as she disappears within the jungle.

There are roosters and chickens roaming the yard and wind chimes that sing with the cooler February breeze. Everyone swears they're made out of driftwood and *not* bones, but I still have my doubts. But they play a pleasant enough song.

I inhale deeply as we walk through her garden. The flowers on some of the citrus trees are blooming and the air is as sweet as Abuela's perfume. One of the orange trees is bursting with fruit, and without even

turning around, Mrs. García nods her approval for me
to try one.

Only one!

It's nice to be friendly with Mrs. García and not have
to steal avocados or lemons from her anymore. (It's a long
story.) She stops every few feet to check on a plant, and
murmurs to them about their water consumption or new
bugs. She sprays some of them with a concoction that
smells like peppermint soap.

She never stops to explain what she's doing, but simply
expects me to follow along and absorb all the information
silently, like the plants drinking up the minty soap and
water. She's not loud and pushy like Caro, but she's
definitely bossy in her own way. She plucks a green bean
and insists I eat more vegetables if I want to keep running
around for no good reason. She points at some unknown

herb and says that if I dry and crush those leaves with eggshells, I'll never get another pimple like the one I currently have on my chin.

Mom's always telling me to be respectful of my elders, and I get it, but old people have no filter.

I pause beneath a familiar tree. "What happened to all of your avocados? Is someone else taking them? Because it wasn't me."

Mrs. García's raspy laugh rattles. "No están en temporada," she says. She points at one of the small green ones I didn't notice among the leaves. "They are still growing."

In all my time nicking fruit off my neighbor's tree as a Miami kid rite of passage, I never really stopped to think about how plants aren't always in season. It may feel like summer all year long here, but the same flowers don't bloom all year.

Mrs. García stops in front of the seeds I planted a couple of months ago. She gestures at the plants they've grown into and proudly commands, "Mira."

I'm looking. And I'm horrified.

"Broccoli?" I exclaim. "I grew broccoli? But I *hate* broccoli. It stinks up the whole house!"

Mom was on a meal-planning kick when she was dealing with the chaos of college and newborn Lucas, and every Sunday she would cook up a bunch of chicken and rice— which are both fine—but then she'd steam broccoli, and that always smelled worse than Lucas's diapers.

"I cannot believe I grew broccoli! Of all the vegetables! I'd take anything else. A tomato, even."

Mrs. García rolls her eyes. She looks impatient with me now as she switches to English. "This is not the season for tomatoes, you ungrateful girl. Come back in the summer and you can grow tomatoes, but for now you take your stinky broccoli."

I stop on my way out of her yard. Looking for a bright side, I ask, "Does broccoli help with pimples, by any chance?"

But Mrs. García has already disappeared.

I love a holiday that gets you out of school, but if they're not going to offer us the gift of sleeping in, the very least they can offer is a pizza party. A movie in the afternoon! A themed arts and crafts activity! I'd happily take a classic pajama day.

But Valentine's Day offers no such break. There are still math tests and homework due. And even worse than that, the day is a roller coaster of weird expectations

and awkward interactions. Classes are interrupted by flower and candy deliveries that leave everyone on high alert.

It's during fourth period when the dreaded

deliveries start. Everyone is watching the door, waiting. No one is listening to Ms. Pérez even though art is arguably the best class. I didn't get anything last year and I don't expect a delivery this year. I don't even want one. The idea of having to carry one of those flowers around all day is super embarrassing. Having everyone guess who sent it to you? No, thank you. I just want to get this ridiculous, very un-pizza-party-like holiday over with.

The door finally opens, and I recognize Shelly, an eighth grader from Future Leaders. She has a cart of flowers and candies.

Ms. Pérez, delighted by the ritual, lets her do the deliveries. And I can't figure out why I feel so nervous as I watch Shelly call out names and hand out the sappy gifts. I know that I'm not getting one. I don't even want one.

Who needs a bunch of flowers when you have broccoli? I repeat it to myself as Shelly walks right past me.

"Vanessa Ramos."

I turn around, surprised. I forgot that I had art with the new girl. She sits at the table behind me, next to the

window. I watch as she's handed a bunch of flowers. Her eyes grow wide and surprised. She hasn't even been at our school for a month yet and she's already getting flowers. I tell myself I'm not going to wonder who sent it. Unfortunately, I'm nosy and can't help but glance at the note that comes with it.

★ CHAPTER 7 ★

I book it to the cafeteria the second we're released from class. I *need* to get there first. I don't even stop to grab a tray as I hurry straight to our table.

Zoey arrives next. "Where's your lunch? It's quesadilla day." Her frown turns worried. "Are you okay? You look sick."

Before I can say anything, Julian—the secretive,  sneaky Romeo in question—sits down with his tray. He dives right into his chicken. Zoey and I stare at him until he finally looks at us.

"What?" he asks, his mouth full.

There's ketchup on

his chin. He still dips everything and anything he eats in globs of ketchup, just like he did back in elementary school. He's still the same kid, except now he's also sending girls flowers and love notes.

"What?" he asks again in our silence.

"I have fourth period with Vanessa," I tell him, and his eyes get wide. "Carnations, Julian? *Really?*"

He shrugs, but he definitely looks sweaty and embarrassed. "We saw the poster about them outside the library and she mentioned never getting any at her old school."

"I've never gotten any!" I snap.

Julian looks confused. "Did you . . . want one?"

"Of course not." And I don't want one. Not from Julian. Or anybody. But *still*. First, he invites someone new to our table, and now he's getting caught up in the dating hysteria going around. I don't want things to change again. That's *not* the plan.

"I just thought it would be nice," he explains. "It's hard being the new kid and she was homeschooled for the past two years. It's not a big deal."

"It feels like a big

deal," Zoey says thoughtfully, her quiet voice almost a whisper.

"Because it is a big—"

Julian elbows me hard just before Vanessa takes a seat. She still has her carnations. She glances at Zoey and me, then smiles shyly at Julian. "Thank you! It's so nice, I love it."

Julian's face is as red as the ketchup still on his chin. "You're welcome."

I've never seen Julian blush, and *that* feels like a pretty big deal.

At home, Dad and Mom are getting ready for their big date. Mom—fresh from the hair salon—acted very surprised when Dad told her he was taking her to some fancy rooftop restaurant that serves incredible Japanese food.

Caro is a nervous wreck as she gets ready for her date with Alex. I've been home for all of ten minutes, and I've seen her race in and out of her room wearing six different outfits.

"What if she puts all those clean clothes in the hamper?" I ask Abuela in an attempt to stir up some trouble.

Abuela's eyes widen at the seventh outfit and she calls after Caro, "¡Esos no están sucios!"

Everyone is losing their minds, but while Abuela has her suspicions about whether pizza should actually be considered dinner, with Mom and Dad headed out on their date and Caro off to get locked in an escape room for fun, Abuela is ordering a large cheese and pepperoni for the anti-Valentine's crew.

After dinner, I grab my laptop to play *BioBuild*. It's been my favorite game since fourth grade and out of everyone  at school, Julian is the only one who still plays regularly. We play online together most weekends. As I log on, I nervously chew my thumbnail, waiting to see his name.

magpieOfmischief: heyyyy

roboJellybean: hey

magpieOfmischief: abuela ordered us pizza, it's a miracle!!

roboJellybean: whoa

roboJellybean: pizza night at the diaz house

magpieOfmischief: yeah everyone else is out on their dates

magpieOfmischief: gross

magpieOfmischief: at least vday is almost over

magpieOfmischief: what a joke of a holiday

roboJellybean: I guess

 I start to type an apology for earlier and for being weird about the flowers and not telling him about the glob of ketchup on his chin, but I can't figure out what to say. I delete my message and restart it so many times that before I can hit send, he writes back.

roboJellybean: gotta go, see you Monday

On Saturday morning, Abuela comes into my room to wake me up even before my school alarm. It has me rethinking this track business. After-school practice and meets are one thing, but having to also wake up early on the weekends is rough.

I'm a little nervous. I'm doing the triple jump today and I've only practiced those a handful of times. Oh, and my whole family is coming to the meet to watch me.

The meet is at a local high school's track. I warm up with some of my other teammates out on the grass. Some of the sixth graders look nervous, but the eighth graders are snacking on chips and taking pictures while gassing one another up. I blow out a shaky breath and try not to let my nerves get the best of me.

I watch some of the other events and root for my teammates. Sammy crushes the mile run. The announcer calls for the 100-meter dash and I hurry over to check in.

"You got this, Maggie!" The shout comes from the stands and even without looking I know it's Caro. I'm very used

to her shouting at me about running. As I get assigned to heat three, I notice Caro slip through the crowd watching us. She leans against the railing to get closer. "Don't forget that it's all about the start."

"Oh my gosh, please stop," I hiss up at her.

"Also watch your form."

"Go. Away," I bite out. But as I get into my starting formation, I can't help but glance over to check with Caro. She's *not* my coach, but she is my very fast sister.

The whistle blows. I take off, but turns out that I *don't* got this, because the two girls on either side of me are just so much faster. It's only my first event, but I'm

BUMP!

still really disappointed. And it doesn't get easier. I knock over a hurdle during the 300 meter and then it takes two tries to make my first high jump.

It's exhausting and embarrassing to mess up over and over. Especially when I can feel Caro watching me from the crowd. Every time I glance up, she's paying attention. It's annoying. But also reassuring for some reason? Don't ask.

"Hey, Maggie!" Sammy calls me over. I stop beside her, Alicia, and Mia Maldonado sitting together on the grass. I know Sammy and Alicia okay, but I don't really know Mia. And I don't know any of them well enough to be teased right now.

Sammy holds up half a sandwich. "You want some? It's a chicken tender sub."

My stomach growls in reply.

They share their food and embarrassing meet stories with me. After we finish eating, the officials announce one of the relays that Alicia is in, and I head over with them. Sammy introduces me to runners from other schools as we stop to cheer Alicia on. And despite mistakes, Caro's shadow, and my humiliating lack of points, it turns out it's kind of fun to be part of a team.

★ CHAPTER 8 ★

On Monday, the entire seventh grade gets to miss sixth period (see you never, algebra!) for an assembly. We file into the gym and I'm relieved to find Zoey almost immediately. I squeeze in next to her and look around for Julian, saving the spot next to me despite Mr. Santiago demanding everyone to fill in all available seating.

I jump up when I spot Julian and wave at him. I can't help the rush of relief I feel when he smiles and jogs over. Lately it feels like I'm a little unsure when it comes to him.

I don't know if he has a crush on Vanessa or if he's just making a new friend from art club. It's different. And I don't expect different and new when it comes to Julian.

But what's great about having two best friends is you balance one another out. Like when I got jealous about Zoey's new band friends last year, I had Julian to help me figure out what to do. And when Julian started to smell like onions in fifth grade, he had me and Zoey to gently point out the importance of deodorant.

"Hey," he says, a little breathless after racing over to us. "What do you think this is about?"

I laugh but he doesn't. I stop when I realize he's serious. "The field trip," I say.

"Oh, right." He nervously taps his bouncing legs.

I'm staring at him, because I can't believe he forgot about the spring break trip already.

"Are you okay?" I ask.

He nods. "Yeah, yeah." He glances around the gym and continues tapping his knees. He rearranges the charcoal pencils in his shirt pocket. He isn't sweating, though, and that's usually an obvious tell whenever Julian is lying or has a secret.

Zoey leans closer to me and whispers, "Are *you* okay?"

Before I can answer, Vanessa sits down on Julian's other side. I hadn't noticed that he'd been saving a seat, too.

"Hey!" Vanessa leans over him to say to us. "Thanks for saving me a seat. Finding somewhere to sit always makes me anxious."

Static rings out from the microphone as Coach Schwartz clears his throat and calls us all to attention.

"Hello, seventh graders! Who is excited about spring break?"

Everyone screams so loud it takes another minute to quiet us enough to hear him again.

As Coach tells us all about the field trip—the fort! Trolley tours! A chocolate museum! Staying overnight in a downtown hotel!—it's like waves of excitement ripple across the crowd. Zoey and I bump shoulders, bouncing in our seats.

"And we expect model behavior at every stop. Let's show everyone how wonderful the students of West Memorial Middle are, okay? And you'll all be picking a buddy for the bus and tours to keep everyone organized."

Buddy? A buddy is one person. A buddy implies a duo. Not a trio.

"It's supposed to be the three of us," I say, crestfallen.

Zoey shrugs. "It's not that big of a deal."

Julian turns toward us. "You two can buddy up for the bus and—" He looks at Vanessa. "I can find someone else to sit with."

My heart is racing. This is not at *all* how it was supposed to go.

Even our school is forcing us to pair off and I *hate* it. It's like the whole world is built for two people. But what does that mean when you have *two* best friends?

Is that possible? Do I have to give one up?

After school, I'm headed to track practice when Zoey comes flying out toward the field. She stops in front of me with a wild look in her eyes.

"What's wrong?" I ask, worried. "Did you miss your bus?"

She shakes her head quickly and then holds up a piece of paper.

A 75 isn't half bad in my world. Especially on an unexpected pop quiz. It's a high enough C that it wouldn't even ruin my grade average. I got an 85 on that same quiz and gave myself a mental high five over it. But for Zoey? I'm not sure Zoey has ever gotten anything below an 89, and even then, she immediately asked to do extra credit before that respectable B+ could have any lasting effect on her progress report.

"This is okay," I tell her.

"No, it's not!" she wails. "My parents will never let me go all the way to Saint Augustine by myself! They'll make me stay home and memorize the periodic table instead!"

"You're not going by yourself. There will be chaperones." At the assembly, they even told us to let our parents know they could sign up to be one.

I shake off the nightmare. My first spring break trip away from home won't be *away from home* if my parents are with me. I love my family, but they know me too well and can sometimes make me feel like such a temperamental . . . baby.

"My parents won't care that there are other adults!" Zoey shakes the quiz again for emphasis.

"This was just a pop quiz before the real test next week. I'll help you study, and you'll turn this C that's already almost a B—"

"No, it's not."

"It's a seventy-five, and if it ends in a five, you round up."

"Maggie!"

"What? That's a legit math lesson!" Having to endure algebra this year makes me really miss fourth-grade math. But now isn't the time to reminisce about simpler days filled with rhymes about place value. Right now I need to remind Zoey that she is honor roll elite. "We're going to turn this into another shiny Zoey straight-A report card before spring break. I promise!"

"I don't know . . ." She hesitates.

I smile wide. "I have a plan."

She doesn't look convinced as she heads off toward the band room.

Down on the track during our warm-up stretches, I try not to worry. It's finally our turn to go on the big spring break field trip, but it feels like my plans are already falling apart. The trip is in two weeks and Zoey's stressed because her parents still haven't signed her permission slip. And on top of that, Julian is acting different and distracted—and is possibly turning into a lovesick zombie like everyone else. When I messed up with Zoey last year, it was because of jealousy over her new friends. I don't want to mess up like that with Julian.

I may not know how to talk about this with Julian, but I can help make sure Zoey doesn't totally freak out.

It's the very least a buddy can do.

✦ CHAPTER 9 ✦

"I won't be fooled. Not this time. Do you hear me?"

It's early in the morning on a Saturday and instead of sleeping in, I'm out planting pumpkin seeds with Mrs. García in her garden. There will be no stinky broccoli this time, but instead some very cute pumpkins to carve in October. Because I'm planning ahead.

"That's how you don't get broccoli," I tell the seeds as I stick them into the fertile soil. "You make a plan and you stick to it." I walk around the garden plot that Mrs. García set aside for me. She said pumpkins need a lot of room. I continue talking to the plants, because that's another one of Mrs. García's lessons. First, I had to learn patience. Now she says I need to become a better listener. I'm not really sure how to listen to plants, but I figure it's probably up to me to start the conversation.

I dust dirt off my hands. "What's my plan, you ask? Great question. My plan is still the same: Have an awesome spring break trip with my best friends."

Seventh grade was supposed to be this perfect time to figure ourselves out. And I did it! But then everyone started changing *again*. Zoey, Julian, and I got our hobbies and clubs, a fun group text, and a designated lunch table. The three of us have been closer than ever. The last thing I want is to lose any of that. I just have to adjust the plan to make sure that Zoey is able to go on the field trip and Julian hangs out with us.

"Of course he'll hang out with us," I tell the seeds as I water them. "We're the terrific trio. No, wait, the timeless triad! The tremendous trinity, the—"

"¡Okay, ya! That's enough talking."

Abuela slips out from between two big banana leaves. One second she wasn't here, and now she is. This backyard is really something else.

"Hola, vecina," Abuela greets Mrs. García. They stop to give each other a quick hug. There's a lingering competitiveness between them, but they were way more combative before Abuela started trying out all these clubs and hobbies and inviting Mrs. García along. They're in a book club at the library now. A magical realism book about inheriting a family curse really brought them together.

I tell Mrs. García and the pumpkin seeds goodbye and that I'll be back tomorrow before heading to the grocery and bakery with Abuela. While she grabs a warm, freshly baked loaf of Cuban bread for breakfast, I stop to chat with Pablo. His guava-red hair is a stressed-out mess, but he looks excited to see me.

"I've been thinking about what you said," he tells me quietly, so that the gossiping viejitos drinking their café don't overhear.

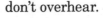

"What did I say?"

"About making a plan to tell my parents about the other job."

"Oh, right!" I lean in and whisper. "What's the plan?"

"I'm going to take them out to eat there. Show them how nice the place is, and *then* tell them."

"That's brilliant, Pablo!" I say, not at all in a whisper. The viejitos all glance over along with some of Pablo's family in the kitchen behind him.

Pablo shoves a pastelito toward me and I hold it up with a big grin. "Brilliant."

After planting pumpkins and my chat with Pablo, I'm feeling super confident when Zoey comes over to my house that afternoon to study. We spread all our science notes across the kitchen table as we get down to work. Zoey figures it might be easier to study at my house since she also lives with her grandparents, parents, and three siblings. That's two extra people than my house, so the math checks out.

Unfortunately, practical things like math don't always apply to my family.

"Sorry," I mutter. "Do you want some headphones?"

Zoey just shakes her head as she leans over her notes. She's in the zone.

I try my best to focus like her, but I get distracted by the itchy ant bite on the top of my foot. I must have gotten it in Mrs. García's garden. The top of the foot is the worst place to have a bug bite.

I lean down and try scratching the bite through my sock. I glance over at Zoey hard at work and stop scratching

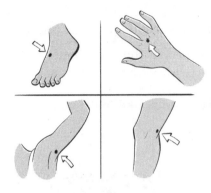

my foot to search around for my pencil. My notebook bumps into it and I quickly reach over to snatch it up before it rolls off the table. Unfortunately, I knock over my water bottle onto Zoey's notebook.

"Thank goodness it's empty," I say with a relieved laugh.

Zoey smiles a little as she continues to work. Her level of focus is incredible.

"My mom would be very proud," I say.

"Your mom would be very proud of what?" Mom asks

as she walks into the kitchen. Her big book of tax laws is under her arm and a pencil is stuck in her mostly secure hair bun.

"Of how hydrated I am," I say.

Mom smirks. "Hello, Zoey. How's your mom?"

Zoey catches Mom up on her family and Mom is smiling big with total stars in her eyes when she notices Zoey's open binder and how organized it is.

When they start talking about different pens, I get up and trudge down the hall to my room to get my laptop. I really hate studying and homework. I can never stay focused. Whenever I'm finally home from school, the *last* thing I want to do is open up my backpack and do more of it.

When I return to the kitchen, Zoey is back to work, Mom is off crunching numbers, and Abuela is serving us a snack of white rice topped with fried eggs.

I dive into my plate as Zoey takes a short break to eat hers. Abuela checks the news on the tablet Dad bought her for her birthday. She can talk to it and ask it questions in Spanish and she loves that she can stream her favorite shows on it.

She has the font set to such a large size, I can read it from here. When a commercial about some cold case murder blares in very dramatic Spanish, Abuela raises the volume even louder and looks at me with wide eyes.

"Abuela . . . that has nothing to do with my field trip."

She makes a face and sighs dramatically like an actress in one of her telenovelas.

Zoey gets back to her notes, so I open my laptop with every intention of logging on to our school website so I can use the resources my teacher uploaded for us . . . but the *BioBuild* icon is right there. And I really want to check and see if Julian is online.

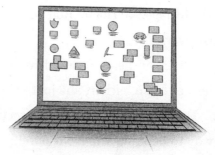

Mom's voice shouts from the other side of the house and I freeze guiltily like I've been caught. But she's not yelling at me.

"*¡Mami!*" she calls out over all the noise of Abuela's tablet. "¡Estamos estudiando!"

Abuela—despite always telling Caro and me that young ladies don't yell in the house— very *loudly* announces that she'll just watch her shows in her house. The back door closes behind her with a mildly annoyed bang. The kitchen finally quiets down.

Until Dad pops into the house with Lucas tucked under  his arm like a football. They're both smiling big. "Guess who almost walked?"

"You?" I tease.

Dad laughs but then stops quickly when he notices all the work around us. "Don't want to interrupt," he says sheepishly. He whispers, "Honor Roll Maggie and Zoey. Taking over the world."

When he heads toward his room, I warn him, "Don't bother Mom, either; she just yelled at Abuela."

Dad smoothly changes direction, spinning the other way to head for the front porch.

I log on to *BioBuild,* but Julian isn't online. I wait for a minute, bouncing my pencil against the table. I scratch my foot again, but that just makes it itch more. Abuela returns inside with a determined look and a stick of lit palo santo in her hands. She swirls it around the kitchen.

I wave my hand in front of my face, batting away the sweet smoke. "Abuela!"

Abuela uses palo santo whenever she does a limpieza.

That means cleansing the space around her or shaking off bad energy.

Palo santo is a sacred tree.

Be responsible about sourcing your palo santo!

"Esta casa necesita una limpieza," my bruja abuela stubbornly says.

"Saint Augustine isn't haunted, and no one needs a cleansing!" The last thing I need is for her to make Mom start worrying about letting me go.

Dad walks past, holding Lucas under his arm again. "This diaper definitely needs a cleaning, though. Ooh, boy, you stink."

Caro's door opens, spilling her loud, whiny music into the rest of the house. Mom shouts about us studying again.

Zoey sighs as she closes her notebook with defeated finality. With a shake of her head, she says, "Your house is as noisy as mine."

★ CHAPTER 10 ★

On Monday, I'm in my seat way before the late bell. I've never been this early to my science class. My pencil is out—nervously tapping my desk—as if channeling Zoey will somehow help both of us when she doesn't even have science until after lunch.

Mrs. Clements checks attendance and then it's go time as she hands us our tests.

Everything Zoey and I went over in our study session suddenly and completely disappears from my memory.

It's like a bubble has popped. I try to focus harder, but that just gives me a headache right behind my eye.

Eerie Eddie glances over at my pencil. I sheepishly stop tapping it against my desk, take a slow breath, and try my best.

Mrs. Clements gives us the rest of class to do a worksheet in our assigned groups as she grades the tests. My pencil starts tapping out a nervous beat again.

"Since when do you get all stressed out about tests?" Eddie asks me.

"Since our field trip lies in the balance." Mrs. Clements is more than halfway through the stack. I try to decode her face and wish my eyes could zoom in to see which test she's grading. But no bionic eyes, unfortunately. I look at Eddie and ask, "You're going, right?"

"On the field trip?" He nods. "Yeah, I'm excited for the ghost tours."

I laugh, remembering Abuela with her palo santo. I'd bet she'd really freak out if I brought Eerie Eddie home with me to study.

I unintentionally let out a shriek and the whole class glances at me.

Eddie frowns. "Are you okay?"

I sink into my seat and offer a quick jerk of a nod. Why in the world am I thinking about bringing Eddie home? I look at him from the side of my eye. He's a total e-boy.

He paints his fingernails and has several earrings. He always wears a black long-sleeved shirt under his school-approved polo uniform, even when it's a thousand degrees outside. He knows how to wear eyeliner when I do not. But when he laughs at my jokes, I feel like the funniest person ever.

My eyes widen. That flip-flop feeling in my stomach is back.

What is this feeling?

"All right, everyone, I've graded your tests," Mrs. Clements calls out. "You can come up to my desk to see what you got when I call your name."

For a split second, I forgot about the science test. *This* is why I have a stomachache. Not because of eyeliner or butterflies.

Eddie glances at me and raises his eyebrows.

"What?" I snap, realizing I'm looking at him again, counting his earrings.

He nods toward the teacher, who calls my name again.

"Oh, sorry!" I jump out of my seat and head up to her desk and see my graded test on top. My 85 from the pop quiz has dropped down to an 80 on the test. Still not bad in my world. But it makes me worry even more about Zoey's grade. This periodic table business is no joke and I'm going to be super mad if all these elements mess up our spring break plans.

As soon as the bell rings, I'm out of my seat, rushing out of the room as my empty stomach and I race toward the cafeteria and a much-needed lunch.

"You got an eighty?" Zoey wails from the other side of our lunch table. She's got all her notes out again, determined to study the cursed periodic table one more time.

"Yeah, but that's, like, really good for me!" I assure her, but she doesn't look convinced. Instead, she looks very, very stressed.

"It's five points lower than you scored on your pop quiz."

I nudge her tray closer to her, so she'll actually eat some of her lunch before we run out of time. I am *such* an abuela. "Yeah, but that doesn't mean you'll get a lower score. Plus, I was distracted by counting Eerie Eddie's earrings. He's got four on one ear, but three on the other. It seems unbalanced, like your head might tip more one way than the other. And then my stomach growled, and you know how I get before lunch."

Zoey looks up from her notes and narrows her eyes at me.

"What?" I look down to see if I have barbecue sauce on my shirt, but I'm good. I stuff another chicken nugget into my mouth.

I gasp, almost choking on the nugget. I take a big gulp of water and then whisper in an offended hiss, "No, I do not!"

"You were counting his earrings." She leans closer, her tone matching mine.

"Because I was distracted! My mind wanders during tests, and wondering why he has an odd number of earrings was more interesting than trying to remember the atomic number of potassium."

"It's nineteen!"

"Really? Huh. I think I got that one wrong." But then it hits me, and I smile with relief. "But you

know it! You're totally ready for the test!"

Zoey doesn't look relieved at all as she flips open her huge, perfect binder and starts slipping her notes back exactly where they go instead of shoving them in whatever folder like I usually do.

"Zoey—" I start to say, but she cuts me off.

"You're going to start going out with Eddie just like Julian is going out with Vanessa and it's going to ruin everything."

"No one is going out with— Wait, Julian is going out with Vanessa? For real? Like officially?" They're a couple? She's his girlfriend? There are way too many questions jumping around in my head. When Julian sits down next to me, I can only stare at him.

"What?" Julian is so startled that his voice squeaks.

Zoey shakes her head. "I'm going to finish studying in the library." She leaves without touching her food. And on chicken nugget day.

"What was that about?" Julian asks me. He looks worried and very confused. "What's going on with her?"

I've never seen Zoey stress out like that. I turn to Julian. "Are you going out with Vanessa?"

"What?" Julian squeaks again. "No! We're just friends." I can't tell if the squeaking is because he's lying or twelve. But it's how I reacted to Zoey's question about Eddie. And he and I are just friends. Right? I study Julian for any telltale sweat, but he's clear. Feeling confused, I grab one of Zoey's abandoned chicken nuggets as I wonder when everything got so complicated. That's when it hits me.

Zoey said this was all Julian's fault.

Because Julian is going out with—or at the very least *wants* to go out with—Vanessa.

And Zoey is mad . . . because she likes Julian!

★ CHAPTER 11 ★

Mom and Abuela pick Caro and me up after track practice to go to the mall. Running helped a little, but I've been stressed all afternoon. Once I'm in the car, I can't wait another minute and text Zoey directly instead of in the group chat. There's no way I'm going to bring up her possible crush on Julian (so weird!) but I really want to know what she got on her quiz.

Unfortunately, she doesn't text me back, which makes me panic.

And the bad news keeps on coming, because I've just been told that Abuela has officially signed up to be a chaperone for my field trip.

"You've got to be kidding me!" I wail from the back seat.

Mom ignores me, cursing under her breath in Spanish as she fights Miami traffic and road construction.

"¿Por qué yo no puedo ir?" Abuela asks me from the front seat.

"You can't go because you said Saint Augustine is haunted! Why would you even want to go there?"

"Y tu dijiste que no está embrujado," she volleys back before returning to her audiobook. She not only has time to dog walk, join a dance class, and lead a book club, but she's going to chaperone a school field trip. I take it back. I was a terrible influence on her.

Caro laughs beside me. "She's got you there. You kept saying it's not haunted so now you can't use that as a reason for her not to go."

"The *reason* for her not to go is because it's a trip for seventh graders."

"*And* their chaperones." Caro grins at me. "Which now includes your abuela."

Zoey's panicking about the test . . . because she's got a crush on Julian . . . who has a crush on Vanessa . . . and now my abuela is going to Saint Augustine with us? This was *not* the vibe I had planned for our field trip. This trip is meant for the tremendous trio to be free from our strict parents and annoying siblings. It's our time to be goofy tourists without our families showing up to embarrass us.

Mom hits the brakes hard, saying a word I am not allowed to say in Spanish *or* English. I grab my phone and slip on my headphones to listen to music. DJ Junior Peña finally has a new song out, and while it's not as popular as the last one, I think it's my favorite.

We're headed to the mall because I need an actual suitcase and new sneakers for my trip. And because Caro is on a mission to find the perfect prom dress.

It takes forever to find a parking spot before we can finally head inside one of the big department stores that always smell like old lady perfume. I find a suitcase in under ten minutes, with wheels and everything. I'm a very speedy shopper. I'm also very hungry and Mom promised me a pretzel when we're done.

What kind of magic makes a mall pretzel so good?

But unfortunately, Caro is still searching through the racks of dresses and I get stuck waiting by the fitting room for her to finish. It's going to be a while because she's already tried on seven different dresses and none of them have been the mysterious perfect dress she's searching for.

"This is taking forever," I complain loudly.

"Tranquilízate," Abuela murmurs.

I would love to calm down, but Caro is now on her eighth dress.

"Prom is a big deal," my sister says as she turns around in front of the mirror.

"Well, mall pretzels are a big deal to me," I argue. I don't understand why she's so nervous about a dance. She's been to them before. "And you're only in the eleventh grade. You still have next year's prom." I make faces at her from behind her back, but thanks to the three-way mirror, she sees me and scowls.

"I'm going to prom with another girl. It's a big deal and I want to look amazing."

"¡Tu va a ser la más hermosa!" Abuela sings out.

I roll my eyes. "I bet Alex will be prettier."

"Everyone will be gorgeous," Mom cuts in, and hands Caro a sparkly red dress. My sister's eyes light up and she rushes back into the fitting room. Mom turns toward me. "Leave your sister alone." She gives me a calculating look. "Don't you also have a dance coming up?"

Before I can lie or distract her with more pretzel talk, Caro shouts from inside of the fitting room, "Yes, she does! The seventh-grade dance!"

I am suddenly cornered by four Moms and four Abuelas thanks to the huge, evil mirror.

I don't want to talk about the dance, especially not when I'm surrounded by sparkly dresses and feeling dangerously low on sugar.

"I'm not going."

"Why not?" Mom asks.

Caro, still in the fitting room, calls out, "No date?" Not only is my sister not helping, but she is as loud as the rest of us.

"No," I argue with the closed door. And because I'm annoyed at how young she makes me sound, I add, "I could have one if I wanted."

I immediately regret this overconfident outburst.

Abuela's eyes light up. "Maggie! ¿Tienes un novio?" There goes Abuela and her novio alarm. "El niño . . . ay, cómo se llama . . . Julian!"

GROSS!

"Julian is *not* my boyfriend! He's just my friend. And he's barely even that these days now that he's going out with the new girl."

"Oh! Julian has a girlfriend?" Mom asks, sounding curious.

"He *says* they're not going out, but who knows anymore. Zoey likes Julian, who likes Vanessa, and I still don't know how to wear eyeliner!" I cross my arms and fall back in my chair

JULIAN IS THE
WORST!

☐ Always late to lunch

☐ Never plays Bio Build anymore

☐ Sent new girl a flower

☐ Making Zoe all stressed out

in a huff. "The world is upside down."

The door opens and Mom and Abuela whirl toward Caro and gasp. Even I have to admit that the dress is really pretty on her. She spins in front of the mirror to Mom and Abuela's applause. When she looks at me, her smile turns into a smirk. "Do you *want* to wear eyeliner?"

"No," I say, without sitting up. "I want a pretzel."

Caro rolls her eyes toward the ceiling and something about it reminds me of Mom. Like she walked into the fitting room as my obnoxious, terrible sister, but walked out a patient, all-knowing grown-up. All thanks to a dress and cursed mirror.

"New things are scary, and nothing ever prepares us for our first crush," she says patiently.

She's not wrong, but I don't tell her that. I'm not even the one with a crush, but nothing could have ever prepared me for Zoey liking Julian. The three caballeros! The trustworthy trilogy! *This* is why I don't care about the dance. Because dances aren't about friends. They're about couples and dresses and dancing super close. Everything's already a mess. A dance is the last thing we need.

"Also, this dress was left on the hook in the fitting room and I'm pretty sure it screamed your name," Caro says.

Maggie! Maggie Diaz!

I don't need a dress because I'm not going to the dance. I'm not even all that into dresses.

But I want *that* dress.

We trudge on to the shoe department. It only takes me five minutes to find a comfortable pair for my trip, but Caro has to find fancy heels that match her dress and Abuela is trying on *all* of them to figure out which will work best for her dance class. They're going to start ballroom next.

Finally we escape from the rows and rows of aisles and different departments and make it to a blessed register, where Mom buys the suitcase, shoes, and dresses. As the cashier scans the blue dress, Mom doesn't tease me about wanting it even after I was so adamant about not going to the dance. And then I finally get my prize of a pretzel and it's everything I dreamed, because nothing beats a mall pretzel.

When I get home, I hang the dress in the very back of my closet and do my very best to never think about it again.

★ CHAPTER 12 ★

I race to school the next morning to find Zoey. I don't even stop to eat breakfast—much to Abuela's horror—but it's not until I park my bike beside the band room and hear the instruments that I remember jazz band practices in the morning now. I stop in front of the door's window and search the room for Zoey but don't see her anywhere.

I tell myself I'll catch her in algebra before I race to homeroom.

In first-period social studies, Mr. Khan assigns us a worksheet that's just a word jumble of places in Saint Augustine and it hits me that spring break is *next* week.

I'm pretty sure all our teachers are just as ready for some time off. We get to play games in PE—which would have been even more fun with Zoey but she got to miss because of practice for honor band—and then, after yesterday's science test, Mrs. Clements plays a documentary about penguins. The whole morning is a breeze, but I want it to hurry up and be over because I'm anxious to get to lunch so I can *finally* talk to Zoey.

But it's only Julian at our table when I get there.

Julian doesn't know why Zoey was mad at him. And he *definitely* doesn't know that she likes him. Julian used to love to remind us that *communication is key*, but now I'm caught in the middle with the secret to end all secrets. I need to get us back on track.

"My abuela signed up to be a chaperone for the field trip."

Julian's face softens with a small smile. "Hey, you'll be roommates again."

"Ugh, don't remind me."

"My parents can't go," he tells me. "But Vanessa said her mom is going to be a chaperone, too." Now he's smiling the way Caro does whenever she's on the phone with Alex. Or talking about Alex. Or is remembering something Alex said.

I glance around for Zoey. The last thing she'll need to see is Julian getting all heart-eyes over Vanessa.

"Vanessa isn't here today—"

I'm relieved it'll just be the original three today.

"But she told me she saw my mural and loved it," Julian goes on. "She's way smart and—"

Julian's face falls. "Wait . . . what?"

He hasn't been to science class yet to watch the documentary. "It's true." I shrug. "Fun fact."

"That's not fun," he says with a shake of his head. "It's gross."

I spot Zoey talking to Maya and some of the other band kids and nearly jump out of my seat. I wave my arms and call out her name. She nods in acknowledgment, but it takes her another minute to walk over.

"Sorry," she says. "Band practice ran over and our director brought muffins."

"I've been texting you since yesterday." I'm nearly vibrating in my seat and can't wait another second. "Did your parents sign the permission slip after you aced the science test?"

"I didn't," she says after a sigh.

"You didn't what?"

"I didn't ace the test."

"Oh," I say, worry creeping into my voice, but then I snap out of it. She probably just got one or two questions wrong. "No worries, you can—"

"Enough, Maggie!" Zoey says suddenly. "Enough with the forced positivity and plans and everything else! I failed the science test, okay? I mixed everything up and I didn't see your texts because my parents have my phone, and I officially can't go on the field trip."

The outburst is so unexpected my mouth snaps shut. A million thoughts happen at once. They take off in my head like buzzing bees. There's disbelief and panic and crushing disappointment. But I'll deal with them later. The most important thing right now is Zoey.

"Julian can be your bus buddy," Zoey mumbles after a minute.

Julian looks guilty. "I already asked someone else."

Before he can say Vanessa's name—disappointing Zoey even more—I assure her, "Don't worry about me. I'm very flexible with change."

Despite everything, Zoey laughs.

*　　*　　*

There's no time to process that my dream field trip fell apart, because I only have four days to find a bus buddy and roommate. And I have to find *somebody* because the alternative is a total social nightmare.

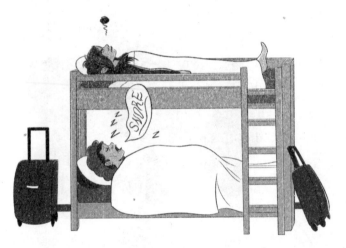

I refuse to be roommates with Abuela again.

At track practice I ask Sammy, but of course she's already buddied up with her best friend, Alicia. Caro barks at us to break it up and keep running. I make a mental note to steal one of her shirts.

By Friday, it becomes apparent that everyone already has someone. This whole pairing-off business has cursed me again. The only other loner I know is Eddie, and there's no way I can ask him.

"Why not?" Zoey asks me in the locker room after we change for PE.

"Because," I say like that's answer enough. "He's a boy." We head toward the track. "And even if I did ask him to be bus and trip buddies, I'd still have to be roommates with Abuela." I slow down to glance through the window into Mr. Khan's class. Eddie has social studies this period.  I realized this by total accident when I happened to look in that window every time we walk out to the field.

I try to ignore the nervous flutter in my stomach. This is my last day to find someone.

"Well, make sure you take lots of pictures," Zoey says, and guilt hits me again. It isn't fair that she's missing the field trip.

"I'm so sorry you can't go," I tell her. "We will *never* study at my house again."

She laughs as she bumps her shoulder against mine. "I didn't realize how stressed out I've been about school and the trip and . . . everything."

Vanessa comes over to us. "Hey, mind if I walk with you?"

"Sure," Zoey says.

"Who says we're going to walk the mile?" I say with a little bit of attitude.

Zoey tells Vanessa, "Don't mind Maggie. She's on the track team and takes running very seriously now."

I need to be protective of Zoey. Especially now that she likes Julian but can't go on the field trip with us. We set off together at a slow jog as Zoey chats with Vanessa about band and the latest book we had to read for English. When Vanessa mentions the field trip, Zoey admits she can't go.

"That's such a bummer," Vanessa says, and sounds genuine.

"Yeah," Zoey agrees, and slows down. "My mom almost had a heart attack. She says the last couple of years of school have been tough and put a lot of pressure on me. She wants me to rest for spring break." Zoey shakes her head. "Shocker, I know, but it sounds way better than memorizing the periodic table."

"My mom is super protective, too," Vanessa says, matching Zoey's pace. "The only reason she's letting me go to Saint Augustine is because she is a chaperone."

I mutter, "Relatable."

Zoey suddenly stops. She looks from me to Vanessa and I don't have enough time to stop her before she says, "You two should be buddies for the trip."

Mom picks me up after track practice. "Nervous?" she asks me on the ride home.

I wipe sweat from my face and hairline. "No, not really. I mean, I still need to work on the high jump, but don't tell Caro that."

"I meant about your field trip."

"Oh! No, I'm excited." My chest gets all warm and tense. I twist the towel in my hands. "I'm disappointed about Zoey not being able to go, but I'm going to room with Vanessa, the new girl."

Mom nods. "I think you can stop calling her the new girl by now."

"Yeah, I guess."

After dinner, Mom catches me shoving clothes into my new suitcase and decides to help me pack. Being an organized packer apparently just means putting all your stuff into a bunch of smaller bags.

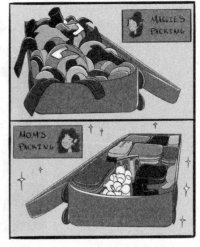

I can't help but ask, "How old were you when you went on your first trip away from home without your parents?"

She folds my socks into tiny squares. "Eighteen," she says with a laugh. "When I left for college."

Eighteen? And here I am getting ready to go somewhere without mine at only twelve. I swallow hard and shove my deodorant and emergency just-in-case pads into the toiletry bag Mom gave me. I haven't started my period yet, but at twelve, I'm on guard. Mom watches me as she slips the small bag neatly into the corner of the suitcase. "But Caro went on her seventh-grade trip at twelve, too."

"Yeah, and she got to go to *Orlando*."

At least Mom isn't as worried about me going on this field trip now that Abuela is going to be chaperoning. "And it's very okay to feel nervous," Mom says in her soft, careful voice. It's her baby voice, the one she uses with Lucas.

"I'm not nervous!"

And I'm not. I'm *excited*. This field trip is the biggest deal ever and I can't wait to get out of this town that I've never left. It's just that nothing is how I wished and planned. Zoey isn't going and now I'm roommates with someone I barely know. And if my stomach starts to hurt again? It's probably just because I didn't eat all my dinner. Abuela made potaje today, which, no matter what she says, is basically black bean soup and *not* my favorite.

After I finish packing, I slip out of my room and find

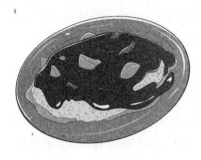

my parents in the living room. It's their Friday movie night. They both laugh and the sound relaxes the knots in my stomach. Since I'm still hungry, I squeeze in between them on the couch to steal some of their popcorn.

★ CHAPTER 13 ★

We have to be at the school no later than 8:00 a.m. Monday morning because the buses are leaving at 8:30 sharp. This is according to our teachers, the forms they sent home, and the texts our parents received Friday afternoon and *again* on Sunday morning. But for the first time in my entire school life, I don't need a reminder, alarm, or even an early bird Abuela to wake me up. Because by some internal clock miracle, I'm up by 6:00 a.m.

Abuela's never been prouder of me.

Abuela is humming and dancing around the kitchen as she prepares her coffee. She's so excited, like this is some vacation for her. I can't help

GRUB GRUB GRUB

but wonder how much chaperoning she's actually going to be doing.

"Abuela, you know you have to, like, watch us, right?" I finish off my toast and around the last bite say, "Like a chaperone."

"Claro," she says. "Tengo que protegerte de los malos espiritus."

I'm pretty sure protecting me from bad spirits was not on the list of tasks she was given when she volunteered to accompany my seventh-grade class. Abuela announces that coffee is made just before my frazzled mother flies into the kitchen.

"Wake up, Maggie!" Mom calls out before noticing me. "You're going to be—"

Her eyes widen when she spots me at the table, already dressed and ready to go.

Outside, birds are chirping, and is it just me or does the air smell better than it does on a school day? I skip over to the car, the most excited I've ever been to head to my middle school.

Mom asks a hundred questions about the hotel and our trip itinerary the whole way there. She sounds nervous—which doesn't surprise me—but she's mostly worried about Abuela, which does.

"I'm sure she's old enough to look both ways before she crosses the road, Mom."

Mom ignores me as she asks Abuela if she brought all her medicines. "The blood pressure one, too?"

"Ay, sí, niña," Abuela huffs.

We get to school, where the parking lot is busy with buses and parent drop-off. It's funny seeing us all together at school in regular clothes instead of our uniforms. Mom helps me get my small suitcase out of the back of the car.

"You packed your toothbrush after you used it this morning, right?"

"Yes, Mom."

"And you have your phone?"

"Always."

Mom lingers like she's not quite ready to let me go. She yanks me close for a quick hug and kisses the top of my head. "I'll get out of here so you can go on your big trip."

When she steps over to Abuela and presses her cheek to hers in a goodbye kiss, murmuring something in Spanish, I try not to roll my eyes. My big trip . . . with my abuela. We both wave goodbye as Mom drives off. Once she's gone, I look back toward the lines by the bus and it hits me again that Zoey won't be here.

My eagerness sinks into guilt and disappointment again. Whenever I imagined this morning, my nerves hadn't stood a chance against my excitement. I see familiar groupings and duos lining up for the bus and sigh, feeling a little jealous and a lot alone. Abuela nudges me forward.

The buses aren't like the regular yellow school ones. They're those big travel ones I sometimes see throughout Miami shuffling tour groups around the city. I lean up on my toes to try to peek through the windows to the inside of the bus. There are plush seats in rows of twos. So much fancier than a regular bus!

"Hey, Maggie! Nervous?" Vanessa asks me.

"No!" I say immediately. And then quietly ask, "Why? Are you?"

Vanessa nods. "I haven't been on a trip in forever," she says, then smiles. "But I'm excited!"

A teacher takes our suitcases and bags before we line up to get on the bus. Cool air hits me from a vent in the ceiling and I imagine this is what getting on an airplane feels like. I don't know, of course, but it's fun to pretend.

Vanessa's mom and Abuela sit up front with the other teachers and chaperones. Vanessa and I move farther down before we pick our seats. She offers me the one by the window.

I look around for Julian. In all the stress of Zoey not being able to go, I never asked Julian who his bus buddy is. Vanessa takes out her phone and earbuds. She offers me one just as I finally spot Julian coming up the middle aisle toward us. I freeze when I see who he's walking beside.

When did they become such good friends? Julian waves and jumps forward to grab the seats in front of us. Eddie looks early-morning sleepy. He nods at me before dropping down into his seat by the window and slipping in his own earbuds. It's starting to feel warm with all these people getting on the bus now, so I check the AC vent above us. Julian leans over the back of his seat and I scoot closer to him.

"Eddie's your bus buddy?"

"Yeah," he says. "My roommate, too."

"I can hear y'all," a grumpy voice says from the seat right in front of me.

"I was just curious," I return. "Also whispering."

Julian shakes his head. Eddie says, "You don't really have a whisper voice."

I fall back in my seat and wish I could text Zoey. But if I could, would she feel jealous that she's not here, too? This first field trip business is already a mess.

The thing about never having been anywhere farther than Palm Bay is that a long bus ride very much *feels* like a long bus ride. My phone's battery is about to die after watching a bunch of my favorite streamer's *BioBuild* gameplay videos. But I can't read like Vanessa because I didn't bring a book, and even if I did, reading in a car always makes me feel carsick. On the tiny TV above the chairs there's some cartoon movie sequel playing. The busy interstate outside the window doesn't offer much distraction, either.

"Where's Zoey?"

Surprised, I glance up. I look at Vanessa, but she's still reading. And that voice sounded like Eddie's, but when I look above the seat, I don't see him. Until I lean closer to the window.

"I figured you would be roommates," he says.

"She couldn't come," I tell him in my not-really-a-whisper voice. I glance at Vanessa beside me. I miss Zoey, but I also don't want to be rude or make Vanessa feel like I don't want to be her roommate. I turn back to Eddie as curiosity gets the best of me. "I didn't know you and Julian were friends." After I got into that awful fight with Zoey last semester, I sat with Eddie a few times at lunch. Julian made his way over a couple of times and they were friendly, but I figured I was the common denominator. I had no idea they were hanging out without me.

"I asked if he wanted to room together," Eddie says. "Figured he'd need one since you'd be with Zoey."

It makes me feel a hundred times better to hear that Zoey, Julian, and I were a foregone conclusion to him.

Of *course* we'd all hang out. We're the three caballeros. But it makes me remember how Eddie wasn't always a loner. He used to have a best friend, too. Miguel Mejia.

6th Grade

But Miguel moved last year. Which means Eddie's had to navigate the total weirdness of seventh grade without his one best friend. And here I've been stressed about having two.

★ CHAPTER 14 ★

After six long hours—except for the one rest stop break we took for lunch back in Orlando—we finally reach the hotel. As soon as the bus stops, everyone scrambles to get closer to the windows. We're all talking over one another until Mrs. Giles returns from checking in at the front desk. She's standing at the front of the bus with her serious face on and it's enough to make us all quiet down.

"I want you all to remember that we are not the only guests at this hotel. We will be mindful of our volume, voices, and valuables."

Mom made me put my souvenir and snack money in a small zippered bag that's strapped around my waist and tucked beneath my shirt. It was a compromise, because at first, she was going to have Abuela hold it for me.

"There will be chaperones to help you get your bags, direct you through the lobby, and get you to your floor, where they will help you find your rooms. Everyone will meet back in the lobby in one hour for dinner before our first tour."

I'm practically bouncing in my seat, ready to go after so many hours. Also, I *really* have to use the restroom.

But we have to wait until they dismiss us by our names and room numbers, and it's taking *forever* for Mrs. Giles to call Vanessa and me.

"Come on, *D* for Diaz," I mutter as my legs bounce in my seat.

"Maybe they're going by my last name?" Vanessa offers, and I'm too embarrassed to admit I'm blanking on her name. Ruiz? Santos? She looks at me sideways and says, "Ramos," like she could tell I was struggling to remember.

Eddie and Julian get called and Julian leaps out of

his chair. Lucky. He spins around and tells us, "See you inside!" I offer him a thumbs-up. Eddie gives me one of those silent head nods again.

When Vanessa and I finally get called, she hops up just before I fly down the middle aisle.

Our hotel room is *amazing*.

I shove my clothes into my half of the dresser. I guess I could just leave it in my suitcase like Vanessa, but what's the fun in that? For the next three days, we get to pretend we live here. Maybe this is what it will be like for Caro when she goes away to college and lives with some roommate she's never met before. I've overheard Caro mention that she's mostly applying to schools in Florida and a couple in other states. She got really excited about one in Atlanta. I can't wait until she's out of the house. I won't have to fight her for the bathroom in the morning or listen to her very loud and very terrible music from the other side of the wall. I can run track in peace without her trying to "coach" me.

I close a drawer, then ask Vanessa, "Are you going to go to college?"

She looks up quickly, like she's surprised I'm talking to her. We didn't really talk on the bus. I *should* be a better buddy, but there's this other tiny but loud voice in my head telling me that being nice to Vanessa is somehow betraying Zoey.

"I don't know about college. Maybe some

business classes, though," Vanessa says. "But my dream is to open up my own cat café."

"A what?"

"You can have tea and also feed the roaming cats that  are up for adoption. My mom went to one when she was in Japan and I've been in love with the idea ever since. I'd love to help cats that are a little hissy, to help them feel safe enough to trust their new home. What about you?"

"I've never been to a cat café."

"No, *college*," she says with a laugh. "Do you want to go?"

The idea of more school makes me shudder. But who knows? I didn't know I liked running until this year.

"I'm not sure yet." I kick aside my now-empty suitcase. "But I do know that I'm starving. Let's go to dinner."

Dinner is in the hotel restaurant, where our class takes over most of the tables. The majority of us are doing our best to mind our voices and volume, but I can tell Mrs.

Giles is writing down some names of our more excitable and hyper classmates.

There are carryout trays on the table in the back, and I hurry to grab one, hoping for rice and steak or chicken. Maybe some macaroni and cheese. But the choices are between ham and cheese, or peanut butter sandwiches, with a bag of chips and an apple or orange. It's no hot dinner plate from the deli. I take a ham sandwich, then spot Julian and Eddie sitting together at a table with some of Julian's art club friends. Before I can head in their direction, Abuela calls me to her table.

Vanessa sits down beside me. Her mother is on her other side. Eating with the chaperones was *not* how I planned on starting this field trip. I bite into my cold sandwich just as Vanessa offers me a small basket of fries.

"Where did you find these?" I ask, excited.

She shrugs and gives me a mischievous smile. I glance guiltily at the adults around us, and Vanessa laughs. "I bought them before I realized we were getting sandwiches."

Vanessa Ramos, future owner of her very own cat café and finder of fries. My roommate is definitely a surprising one.

After dinner, there's a chilly sea breeze that's got a bunch of Miami kids shivering. It's time for our first tour, and with dusk almost upon us, I just know I'm about to explore a spooky lighthouse or overgrown cemetery! And we're getting there in style!

Trolleys are waiting for our group outside the hotel and I'm pretty sure they're the best thing ever. They're like those tiny train rides at malls for kids, but bigger and you get to ride them through an actual city. It's official: I *love* them.

"Where are we going?" I excitedly ask a nearby tour guide. "Graveyard? The lighthouse?"

The tour guide smirks. "Ah, another ghost hunter."

"I've done my research. I know all about how the Casa de Sueños hotel used to be a funeral home."

"Well, you will get to experience many scary stories tonight . . . with historical significance."

Historical significance means old speeches and possible home-work assignments. I'm here for hauntings and a lighthouse that promises the echoing sound of laughter and pirates. Not future quizzes.

"You're into horror?" Vanessa asks me as we get in line for the trolley. Her mom and Abuela are right behind us. I glance around for Julian . . . and Eddie. But mostly Julian!

"I don't want to be scared," I tell her. "I want to be spooked. There's a difference."

Abuela scowls before digging through her bag, prob-ably searching for more salt or some crystals to ward off possible curses.

There are three seats in each trolley row. My excitement fizzles. This would have been *perfect* for Zoey, Julian, and me. I pick a row and Vanessa and then her mom slide in after me. Abuela sits in the row in front of us.

I spot Julian and Eddie and wave them over to our trolley. My eyes widen when they slide in beside Abuela. So. Weird.

"You guys ready to be scared?" I ask them.

"Always," Eddie says.

Vanessa shakes her head. "No, thank you."

Abuela throws an impressed look at Vanessa and then then casts a suspicious, sideways look at Eddie beside her. I can see her taking note of his dark clothes and earrings.

My stomach flip-flops as I start to feel weirdly defensive of Eddie. I really hope Abuela doesn't say  something to him, because I'm not sure if he understands Spanish or not. To distract Abuela, I tell her that I'm hungry.

Our spooky tram tour sets off. We're instructed to take pictures with our camera flashes on to capture the ghosts and apparitions in all their glory. This annoying kid in our class, Braden, turns around and snaps a picture of Eddie.

"I got one!"

Eddie is unfazed as he grumbles a boo at him. Out of the many Bradens in my school, I'm pretty sure he's the worst one.

Our first stop is the Old Jail, which is a popular stop that's busy with other tours. Whenever you look up ghosts and Saint Augustine, the Old Jail *always* comes up, but as our guide shares facts about the terrible living conditions that led to all their infamous ghost stories, it really hits home that this isn't the Haunted Mansion ride. This was a horrifying place where awful things happened to real people.

"This place was terrible," I mumble under my breath.

"Nice places don't get haunted," Vanessa returns.

When the tour guide advises us on what to say to make sure the ghosts don't follow us home, Vanessa and I shout the warning back.

The narrator is going all out with their cold case narrator voice, advising us to get our phones out to take pictures of any spirits we happen to see, but I'm focused on Julian leaning back to say something to Vanessa. She laughs as their heads stay leaned toward each other and they continue to whisper and giggle. Julian, my best friend since elementary school, *giggles.*

My mind is spinning as the tour continues down the road, taking us through some more shadowy corners of town. There's talk of pirates and ghosts and I'm missing it, because I'm worried about something *way* scarier. Zoey's not here so it's up to me to defend her territory. She has dibs on Julian. Vanessa only just moved here, and Zoey has known him way longer. I need to make sure nothing happens between Vanessa and Julian. But . . . if I succeed and Zoey and Julian get together . . . I can't help but worry what all of this will do to our friendship trio.

⋆ CHAPTER 15 ⋆

Our spooky trolley tour stops by the city gates just before sunset. It's even colder now and I can't help but shiver. Thankfully, Abuela isn't beside me or else she would make a huge fuss over el sereno getting me. In case you didn't know, cold evening air is absolutely lethal and just as terrifying as a haunted city.

A cold wind zips through the trolley, cutting right through my jacket, and my body breaks out into another

full-body shudder.

Vanessa's mom turns toward me. "Honey, are you—"

"I'm fine!" I blurt just as Abuela spins in her seat with a suspicious look. "Just . . . scared. You know, ghosts and hauntings." I offer a dramatic shiver and call out to the guide, "Ooh, spooky stuff!"

The tour guide smiles before their expression snaps into a foreboding scowl. "*Very* spooky stuff." They advise us to look out for a little ghost girl waving at us as the evening sky slips into darkness and shadows. The lights on the trolley flicker. I have to say, *if* I was actually scared . . . the aesthetic really lends itself to the story of the place.

We reach our final stop and it turns out to be a wax museum. Our guide announces that we get to disembark and head inside. I'm excited for the chance to explore and also to warm up. The entrance surprises me, because it's a really retro drugstore. And our guide? An old man dressed up like an old-school pharmacist. It's like stepping through a time machine that leads to a museum of wax

people. Bold field trip choice. The whole scene reminds me of one of Dad's episodes of *Doctor Who*.

When the tour starts, I realize why *this* is our stop on the haunted trolley tour. There are a bunch of textbook historical figures. This isn't scary or spooky. It's *school*.

When we reach Beethoven, Julian sighs. "I wish Zoey was here. She would love this place."

I'm relieved to hear him say that. But I can't help but sound a little snarly when I reply, "Nice to know you actually miss her."

Julian frowns at me. "Of course I do. I'm bummed she didn't get to come."

I'm seriously so happy that I'm finally hanging out with just Julian and that he also wishes Zoey was here with us! Which is why I have no idea why the next words out of my mouth are "Not that anyone could tell."

Julian stops suddenly. "Are you mad at me?"

I'm not mad at Julian. At least I don't think I am. But Moody Maggie is being *very* loud.

"It's just nice to hear you haven't totally forgotten about Zoey, our *best* friend."

Julian shakes his head and mutters, "Whatever, Maggie." And heads off to check out the Galileo figure. *Zoey likes you!* I want to tell him, but it's not my secret to tell. Plus, Vanessa walks up to him with her mom, effectively ending our conversation.

I start to get a stomachache as I walk past scientists, soldiers, and centurions by myself. It's the oldest wax museum in the country, and now that I'm alone, it's starting to weird me out. When I look away from one of the figures, from the corner of my eye, it feels like their head turns to watch me go.

"You okay?" Eddie asks.

I'm definitely not. Also, I'm pretty sure I just had a heart attack, but still, I squeak out, "I'm fine."

Eddie doesn't argue but continues to walk beside me. And it's nice to not be alone.

We return to the hotel. Abuela checks our room before saying good night. Other chaperones are doing it to make sure no one brought anything they shouldn't or snuck someone into their room, but Abuela silently checks the corners like she's looking for lost spirits. She also checks the minibar to make sure we haven't indulged in an overpriced soda.

I wait for her at the door, feeling mild embarrassment. Before she finally leaves, she quickly fills her palm with the Florida Water perfume and splashes it over the top of my head, dragging it through my hair.

"Abuela!" I hiss, jumping back from the unexpected baptism.

She ignores me and glances at Vanessa, who's sitting on her bed. To my surprise, she doesn't look weirded out by Abuela's actions.

"¿Quieres?" Abuela asks her, holding up the bottle.

"Oh, you ask her?" I mutter, offended, but also soothed by the familiar smell of citrus.

Vanessa politely shakes her head. "I'm good, but thank you."

Abuela nods once and puts the bottle away. With one last long look at me, like a warning, she says, "Pórtate bien."

I don't plan on getting into any trouble and so I tell her good night. It's my first night away from home and technically my first slumber party with someone who isn't family or Zoey.

I don't want to let my sleepover inexperience show. It's embarrassing how much of a late bloomer I am compared with other kids my age. I never feel this way with Zoey, who also has strict immigrant parents. But I'm at a loss on what to do without my usual modes of entertainment. No laptops or Nintendo Switches. And neither of us have been able to figure out how to get onto the hotel's Wi-Fi from our phones. There's a TV, but it has a bunch of channels and shows I never watch at home.

"This is my first sleepover in forever," Vanessa says.

"Really?"

She shrugs. "Yeah, my mom is kind of a worrier, if you couldn't tell."

Vanessa is dealing with having a chaperoning family member tag along, too. By being roommates, we're saving each other from the horror of rooming with our relatives.

"Yeah, my mom can be pretty intense," I say.

"I'm a formerly homeschooled kid with a Japanese mom who worries about everything and a Puerto Rican dad who trusts no one. I'm lucky I ever get to leave the house."

"Oh yeah? I turn thirteen soon, but my Cuban parents didn't let me have a phone until three *months* ago."

Her eyes brighten. "I lied . . . I've never been to a sleepover."

We both explode with relieved laughter and proceed to spend the next hour one-upping each other on all the stuff we've never done.

Early the next morning, Abuela knocks on our door. I roll out of bed to open it and am not surprised to see her dressed, pressed, and ready to go. She points at her watch. "Good morning," she calls out. Abuela mostly only ever speaks Spanish, but it's not because she doesn't know English. She just chooses to speak Spanish with us because it's important to her that we don't lose our ear for it. But she'll use both with the students and teachers because not every kid from Miami is Cuban, and we don't all speak Spanish.

Last night was really fun, but I can't help but feel caught in the middle. Between Zoey's crush on Julian and

★ Cuban American
★ Speaks Spanish

★ Haitian American
★ Speaks Creole

— From Carribean —
Countries
— Neighbors —

his crush on Vanessa. Between my loyalty to Zoey and this new possible friendship with Vanessa. I desperately need some food, and downstairs I discover my new favorite thing other than trolleys.

Continental breakfasts.

I get two of everything and find Vanessa saving me a spot at a table with Abuela and her mom. I take a seat, and a minute later, when Julian sits down 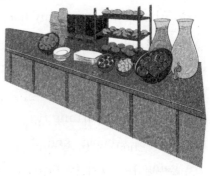 beside me, I have a mouth full of buttery croissants. "Can you believe all of this is free?" I ask him.

"It's not technically free, it's included," he says. "In the fee our parents paid."

"Right, right," I say before I take a bite out of a cheese Danish.

Abuela sips her coffee, then butters a blueberry muffin. I'm a tiny bit embarrassed that we're the only students sitting with their chaperones. But I can handle it. As long as Abuela doesn't—

"Abuela!" I mutter in a flustered hiss.

That's the moment Eddie sits down across from me. When I'm being cleaned like a toddler.

I sink back into my chair and wish I could melt onto the floor. Abuela glances at my horrible posture and rolls her eyes. She then grabs a bunch of napkins (even though I know she has fifty in her bag already) and salt packets and throws them all in her purse before returning to her coffee. Abuela and I are going to have to have a chat about boundaries. Or else . . . I'm calling Mom on her.

We head outside to the waiting trolleys. Figuring I'll sit with Vanessa again, I look around for her when I notice Julian headed toward her. I pick up my pace, but he beats me there.

"Hey," he says. "Mind if I sit with Vanessa today?"

"Sure," I say to my former best friend. I get into the next row back so I can keep my eye on them. And because Abuela is calling my name.

And then, as I'm trying not to be completely obvious about eavesdropping on Julian and Vanessa as they talk about some comic, Eddie sits down beside me.

Now I'm *definitely* caught in the middle.

★ CHAPTER 16 ★

The trolley's speakers crackle just before today's tour guide's excited voice welcomes us to Saint Augustine and we get some fun facts about the city.

It turns out, the city *is* pretty old, but the Spanish and French definitely weren't first. It's the oldest *continuously* occupied city and port established by Europeans, but long before them the Timucua people lived here. Our tour guide shares this when we reach a stoplight and I'm surprised to see Eddie listening intently.

Not that I was watching him.

The trolley reaches our first stop. Castillo de San Marcos.

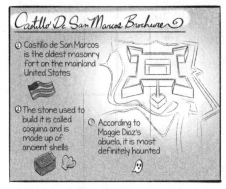

Abuela is already shaking her head and murmuring about all the dark energy around us. She's been hanging out with Mrs. García *way* too much lately.

After checking in at the entrance, our teachers direct everyone to get with their assigned buddies. I jump to Vanessa's side before Julian tries to pull a fast one and steal her. But he's already with Eddie. Abuela and Vanessa's mom have appeared to become chaperone buddies, and together, they gather us into a group. Vanessa and I are with Julian and Eddie as well as Sammy and her best friend, Alicia. There's also Terrible Braden and some kid named Zach who I'm told is not his bus buddy but has been assigned as his tour buddy. A confusing system, but I'm guessing there must be tiers to this field trip buddy situation.

Unfortunately, I can't get out of Abuela's shadow as we walk around the fort. She's supposed to be chaperoning our whole group, along with Vanessa's mom, but her laser focus is directed at me. I can feel it burning the back of my neck even as she stops to read every single informational display, loudly calling me over to do the same.

I'm fine with a well-delivered fun fact, but when she asks me to read yet *another* essay someone wrote on the wall a hundred years ago, I can't get myself to do it. I notice Julian drifting off with Vanessa and the others. Disappointment with a hint of abandonment hits me square in the chest. If Zoey was here, she'd be right beside me.

Am I better friends with her than Julian?

Frustrated, I slink away from Abuela and head over to the seawall. When I hear a weird winding noise I glance over and am surprised to see Eddie. He's standing a few feet away, using an actual camera instead of his phone to take pictures of a sailboat out on the water.

"Where'd you get that?" I ask him.

He looks from me to the disposable camera in his hands. "My mom gave it to me to bring on this trip."

"Very retro," I say, impressed. It is not totally lost on me that I'm complimenting him on this old-school tourist activity when I was just complaining about Abuela

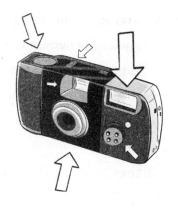

reading every sign in this place.

He shrugs. "My mom's a photographer. She does weddings and portraits." He holds the camera up to his eye to take another picture.

"My mom's an accountant."

Eddie snaps the picture, then winds the camera with his thumb. It clicks and clicks and then he says, "Cool."

Cool. My mom is cool. I, on the other hand, do not feel cool at all. I feel nervous and weird and maybe I ought to be reading those essays with Abuela or tagging along with Julian and Vanessa. And maybe by the way my stomach is now feeling I should not have eaten that extra cheese Danish at breakfast or at least brushed my teeth afterward and—

SNAP!

He winds the camera without looking at me. I feel like I'm stuck in place until our tour guide calls for our groups to meet back in the courtyard. Eddie and I silently head back to the others. As we all meet back up front, Abuela takes those salt packages she stole from breakfast and sprinkles them outside the fort.

When Vanessa and Julian glance at me, I shake my head and tell them, "Don't ask."

Our next stop is across the street at the pirate museum. We each get a map and I figure it'll be something else for Abuela to read, but the guide lets us know that if we pay close attention to the different displays, there's an actual treasure hunt! This is definitely how to get me to read all the signs. Saint Augustine may be historical, but it's also super kitschy and weird. And I'm ready to find

a treasure!

There are artifacts and stolen goods from hundreds of years ago among the interactive displays. I hurry to read all the signs as I look for clues. Abuela is delighted by my touristy enthusiasm when I stop to read the sign she's currently studying. Vanessa sticks beside me as we go head to head against the boys in our group to find the treasure first.

"I see the symbol!" Julian announces too loudly in his excitement. Eddie is surprisingly competitive as he shushes Julian and dashes off to check the clue.

There are puzzles and secret doors. Cannons that we pretend to light and ships we can board. I stand at the wheel and put on my best pirate voice and it's the most fun I've had on the trip so far. After the last clue, Vanessa and I race to the informational desk and show them our completed map just as the boys run up. We get handed our treasure—a plastic toy jewel each—first.

In the gift shop, my little bit of souvenir money is feeling heavy in the zippered pouch Mom made me wear under my shirt and around my stomach. I grab a map and am searching through the eye patches when Eddie stops beside me and reaches for a chef's apron with a Jolly Roger flag on it. When he notices me looking at his selection, he explains, "For my brother."

I didn't even know Eddie had a brother. I hold up the eye patch but think twice about it and put it back. "I'm trying to find something for Zoey. I want it to be fun but not too fun. I don't want her to feel like I'm bragging about the field trip, but she needs to know I was thinking about her." I shake my head. "That didn't make any sense."

"No, it does. Buying souvenirs for other people can be weird." Eddie folds the apron over his arm, then heads over to the barrel of silver rings and bracelets. "How about one of these?"

We dig through the bracelets. I look for black and purple ones because those are Zoey's favorite colors. I notice Eddie picking out some, too.

"Who are you getting those for?" I ask.

"Myself," he says.

I notice he's already wearing some bracelets under his shirtsleeve. It makes me think of his earrings and my next curious question flies out of my mouth before I can stop it. "Why are your earrings uneven?"

"Uneven?" he asks, sounding confused.

"I just meant there are more on one ear than the other."

"Oh." His hand goes to his ear and then simply explains, "My brother pierced my left one too many times."

He looks a little embarrassed now and I feel bad. I hurry to say, "I like it. They're cool. Earrings, I mean. I've had mine pierced since I was a baby. Just the one on each, but I've been thinking of— Hey, Abuela!"

Abuela is suddenly standing right beside me. "¿Dónde está tu dinero?"

My eyes widen as panic sets in. There's no *way* I'm showing Eddie that my money is hidden in some ridiculous purse hidden under my shirt. Abuela doesn't wait for my reply and hurries me away toward the checkout lane. She's quiet but I can't help but feel like that laser gaze of hers is zeroing in on Eddie now. I wonder if his neck is burning? When we get back on the trolley to go to our next stop, Abuela makes sure to sit right between us.

Our last stop of the day is the chocolate factory, where we get the questionable honor of wearing hairnets.

Vanessa's mom takes a picture of us with her phone and then with Eddie's camera. She hands it back to him with a delighted laugh. "It's been forever since I've seen one of those." She turns her phone so we can see the picture she took of us and we crowd around to see ourselves.

We all laugh at how ridiculous we look in these hairnets. I take out my phone and grab a selfie with everyone behind me. My first thought is to send it to Zoey, but then I'm hit by another wave of guilt. Because Zoey's not in the picture. She may not even have her phone back. Sure, I bought her some bracelets, but she's missing out at home while I'm here, bonding with Vanessa.

I save the picture but don't send it.

And then I spend a whole entire tour about making chocolate candy—my third-favorite thing about this trip after trolleys and breakfasts—with a stomachache.

Afterward, I tear off the hairnet and skip the gift shop. I would feel better if I could just talk to Zoey. Reassure her and myself that we're okay and this field trip isn't ruining everything. I head back to the trolley to wait for everyone to finish buying their bags of candy.

"Hey."

I glance up as Eddie slides in next to me with a bag from the shop. Abuela is still in the gift shop. "Not a fan of candy?" he asks me.

"Oh, I'm a big fan, but—" I stop and shrug before saying, "Moody Maggie," like the joke between us is explanation enough.

Eddie nods, then digs into his bag.

The gift reminds me of when he shared his bench and quesadilla with me when I was orphaned at lunchtime. It's so *nice* and not eerie or moody at all. But it's also confusing. Because Eddie's not a Best Friend, but is he a Good Friend? Everyone kept telling me that seventh grade was a perfect time to figure ourselves out, but is it also when we start making all these new friends and crushes?

Not that I have a crush!

★ CHAPTER 17 ★

My stomachache persists through another dinner of sandwiches. But at least things aren't so awkward between Vanessa and me. I still can't tell if she likes Julian like Zoey does or if it's just a one-sided crush on Julian's end. She doesn't talk about him or ask me questions about him. Instead she just asks me questions about stuff I like. I tell her about track and *BioBuild* and then she shows me her sketchbook. It's filled with cats and boba tea, which doesn't surprise me now. She's also drawn some original characters and, well, *us*, which totally surprises me.

"This is so cool," I tell her, awed. She's really good. With a sinking feeling, I admit, "You and Julian really do have a lot in common."

"Yeah," she agrees. "I like his style a lot."

But does she like him? I flip another page and see Zoey's face taking up a whole page. Vanessa takes the notebook back with a shy smile. Her art is just another thing I wish I could show Zoey.

Vanessa jumps over to her suitcase. "I'm going to get ready for bed."

"Oh! Me too," I say, feeling very tired all of a sudden.

For our last day of the field trip, we're finally going to the famous lighthouse (but not at night to ghost hunt, which is disappointing) and the zoological park that has a bunch of alligators. This *is* a Florida field trip, after all. I'm simply grateful to not be subjected to airboats yet again.

But since we're leaving downtown, we're done with the trolleys. I'm going to miss them. Even though it was a confusing game of musical chairs, it was fun way to zip around the city. Now we're back on the buses, and as it turns out, the musical chairs isn't over. Because while I don't have to deal with Abuela attaching herself to my side, I spot Julian stopped by Vanessa.

I point at the seat he's got his knee on. "Are you sitting there?"

He smiles like I gave him permission. "Sure, thanks!"

I should have been more specific. I notice the seat beside Eddie is empty. Before I can even ask, he nods at me.

Why am I feeling so weird about Eddie all of a sudden? Is it because I can't figure out where he lands on the friendship tier? Or is it because I'm feeling so unsure

about Julian, and guilty about Vanessa when I'm worried about Zoey? My friendships were the *one* thing I was always sure about. When did everything get so confusing?

The bus is noisy with lots of different conversations, which makes the growing silence between Eddie and me feel weird. When the lighthouse comes into view, I abruptly ask, "Did you know this lighthouse wasn't the first?"

Eddie turns away from the window. "What?"

"The first lighthouse fell into the ocean," I explain, remembering one of the facts I learned when researching Saint Augustine. "That's why this one is farther away from the coast."

Eddie just gives me one of those silent nods of his before looking out the window again.

What am I doing? I've turned into one of those informational essays on the wall at a museum!

The first lighthouse fell into the ocean. That's why this one is farther away from the coast.

There's a short tour of the first floor's exhibits when we get there. Lots of boat displays and maritime stuff. When it comes time to climb the stairs to the top of the lighthouse, I just barely stop myself from telling Eddie there are, in fact, 219 steps to the top.

What. Is. Wrong. With. Me?

Julian hurries up to me and, right next to my ear, whispers, "This place is way too tall."

Oh, right . . . Julian is afraid of heights.

"Just walk with me," I tell him. "And you probably won't fall."

"Maggie!"

We start up the stairs with Abuela right behind us. I count the steps out loud as we go, but that doesn't seem to be helping Julian relax. So, I opt to distract him.

"I guess," he whispers as we carefully move up the steps together. And then he stops and grabs my arm with a panicked expression. "I don't know!" he admits, his voice cracking with emotion. "Do I *like her* like her? Or do I just think she's a fun new art club friend? And if I *do* like her like her, what does that mean? Do I ask her out? Do I *want* to go out with her? How am I supposed to be someone's boyfriend? My older brother has a girlfriend and now he's failing math. I can't fail math!" His questions and confessions trip over one another as they all rush out of him at once. By the time he stops to catch his breath, we've reached the top of the lighthouse.

My hair whips around in the much colder wind up here.

"Whoa," Julian says when he sees the view. We both freeze as we catch our breath. His arm tightens on mine. "I think I'm going to pass out."

"You're not going to pass out and you're not going to fail math."

I don't know all the answers to Julian's questions. But hearing him ask them in his panicked, squeaky voice makes me feel less alone. I'm not the only one struggling. We both got handed the same surprise pop quiz.

Pop Quiz Questions!
1. Does Julian like Vanessa?
2. Does Zoey like Julian?
3. Does Maggie like Eddie?
4. Is Maggie mad at Julian? NO

It's a relief to be sure of at least one answer. This whole crush business is scarier than being at the top of this lighthouse. It's changing everything too quickly for me to catch my breath. These new dynamics (and new friends) are switching up our established trio.

But whatever their answers are, Zoey and Julian will figure this one out. They have to. But perhaps Caro was right. (I said perhaps!) And Julian hasn't *really* changed or abandoned us. He just needs me to be a better friend right now. Maybe this is like his stinky onion phase all over again.

And being his friend is something I'm very sure of.

After *another* picnic lunch of packed sandwiches, apple slices, and assorted bags of chips, we head to the alligator park. There are some other animals there, but gators are definitely the stars of the show.

Now that Julian is back on solid ground, he's mostly chilled out. He thanked me for listening and made me promise not to say anything to Vanessa. He didn't say to keep it from Zoey, though.

I really need to figure out how to tell Zoey without breaking her heart. I don't want to make everything worse for her. She's going to feel so left out.

Abuela, on the other hand, refuses to be left out.

At least having Abuela glued to my side distracts me from anxiously worrying about my friends. On account of how *embarrassing* it is that she's loudly laughing and cheering her head off over the alligators' antics and the animal trainer's silly jokes. All while wearing an alligator hat she picked up in the gift shop. She keeps trying to get me to wear the matching one.

I shove the hat in the gift bag again. "Abuela, can you please—"

"¡Ay, es como los programas de animales favoritos de tu abuelo!"

My complaint disappears like a popped bubble. The old memory hits me like a sudden wave in the ocean. My abuelo used to love to watch those Saturday-morning wildlife shows. They always came on after my cartoons and he'd sit with me as we learned about pandas, polar bears, and alligators. His favorite were the crocodiles, though. He loved telling me facts about them, like how crocodiles can go a year between meals and live in the water or out of it. Abuelo loved how they could survive almost anything.

I haven't thought about that in a long time.

Remembering those cozy Saturdays at their house makes me see this silly scene in front of me differently.

I suddenly can't help but see the *whole* field trip differently. This isn't just my first time going somewhere without my family.

It's Abuela's first time going on a trip without Abuelo.

Abuela's chaperoning and trying out dance classes and book clubs because she's trying to figure out who she is after losing Abuelo. That's way harder than seventh grade.

And it's definitely something to root for.

CHAPTER 18

We return to the hotel after dinner and I pretty much fall asleep the minute my head hits my nice, cold, fluffy hotel pillow. In the morning, I hit up the beautiful continental breakfast again, where Vanessa and I decide to go for broke and put everything we can on our waffles. She even shares some of the candy she bought at the chocolate factory's gift shop.

After breakfast, we move out of our tiny house of a hotel room, where I say goodbye to everything.

"Goodbye, tiny coffeepot."

"Goodbye, TV with weird channels."

"Goodbye, fully stocked fridge I never touched."

Out in the hall, I sigh. "It was nice while it lasted," I say morosely.

"Yeah," Vanessa agrees. We pat the door goodbye.

We drag our suitcases back onto the bus and hit the road. And just like that, our big seventh-grade field trip is . . . over. Finito. Kaput. Level Complete.

I glance around at the quiet bus. The ride home is less rowdy than the one here. I guess everyone is as tired as me.

It's gray and cloudy and looks like it'll start raining soon. I can sometimes see Eddie's reflection in his window in front of me, but he doesn't turn to talk to me like he did on the way

here, so I mostly watch the passing cars. I can't help from looking at his profile again and again. And the truth of it hits me like a flutter in my stomach.

This whole field trip was supposed to be about making hilarious memories between the three caballeros. The terrific trio. Cue the catchy theme song about being best friends forever! But it didn't work out that way at all. Zoey isn't here, Julian is stressed out about math, and I'm looking at Eddie *again* while wondering what his favorite song is and what it might be like if I was sitting next to him again.

I sink into my seat, feeling a little sick after those sugar-loaded waffles, but mostly just very ready to be home.

I am five steps into our house when I drop my suitcase and melt onto the living room floor with an exhausted groan. Dad laughs and Lucas makes a happy sound as he spider crawls over to climb on top of me.

"How was Saint Augustine?" Dad asks. "Was it as haunted as Abuela feared?"

"¡Sí!" Abuela says just as I whine, "No, it wasn't!"

"Did you have fun?" Dad asks me as Abuela unzips her bag at the kitchen table. She'll be completely unpacked before I even peel myself off the floor.

I definitely had fun even though I am exhausted and it feels like this crush is a heavy thing to carry.

The front door opens and Mom walks inside with Caro, both of them holding takeout bags. Mom grins when she sees

me. "My baby is home, safe and sound." Abuela pouts and Mom goes to kiss her cheek. "You too, Mami."

Abuela waves toward me—still a melted Maggie on the floor but holding Lucas up like an airplane. "Mira a tu hija," Abuela complains, setting a hand on her hip. "Y todos ustedes pensaron que yo sería la que era demasiado vieja para viajar."

"Ay, Mami, ya. Dejar de decir mentiras." Mom rolls her eyes as she goes past her into the kitchen. "No one said you were too old to travel." Mom sets the bags down. I sniff the air and my stomach grumbles. That is definitely not cold sandwiches!

Mom opens the bag and I spring up from the floor. Taco night! We got home just in time.

"So *that's* when Abuela tried to baptize me after a ghost tour."

Everyone is laughing at our stories, even Abuela, who's got plenty of gossip about the teachers and chaperones I mostly try to ignore. She's now decided that she loves Saint Augustine and that we should all travel more. She's also taking it upon herself to plan our next family vacation.

"Speaking of vacations, where are the souvenirs?" Dad leans over to snoop through Abuela's bag. Dad is usually the one coming home from working out of state and he always brings home the best gifts from all the different coastal cities he visits for work. Funky socks from Charleston, South Carolina. Witchy charm bracelets from Salem, Massachusetts. Gummy lobsters from Boston. Abuela and I have a lot to live up to.

Abuela waves me over and I finish the rest of my Jarritos soda—mandarin, my favorite flavor—and jump up to do the honors.

"We begin with our youngest, second cutest, and the only one who drools more than Caro." I duck away from the balled-up napkin Caro just threw at me. "To young Lucas Diaz, we present this plush turtle toy for you to slobber all over.

"Next we have said championship drooler—"

"Mom!" Caro interrupts.

"Maggie . . ."

"Okay, okay. We were going to get you some water from the fountain of youth, but I decided against it seeing as you're already a vampire. Just kidding, Mom! Okay, we got you . . ."

"And now to Dad, it's usually you gifting us tacky and delightful souvenirs from the many ports you've seen, so it is you who we gift . . . a sealed treasure map and your very own pirate eye patch.

"And last but never least, we have Mom. Our

shining star, controller of chaos, and matriarch of math. You are tough and unbreakable, so to you . . . we gift these very cute animal figurines made out of seashells."

Abuela and I get a round of applause. Who knew the silly souvenirs would end up for my family instead of my friends?

After a shower and some unpacking, I pace my room as I call Zoey. When she doesn't answer, my stomach drops. I send her a text letting her know I'm home. I'm anxious to talk to her and make sure she's okay. That *we're* okay. I can't help the hot, twisty feeling of guilt when I think about all the fun stuff I did without her. I grab my laptop to log on to *BioBuild*. It's not a school night, so Mom is letting me play until nine tonight.

Those are weekend hours on a Thursday, people! I love spring break.

Once the game loads there's a moment of excitement when I see Julian's name in my friend's list. And then I remember.

I close my laptop with a sigh. Julian was the last holdout to also play *BioBuild*. I still love this game so much. Him outgrowing it feels like an ending I wasn't ready for.

★ CHAPTER 19 ★

I spend the next day transforming from field trip social butterfly into an introverted caterpillar. I even spin myself  into a silky cocoon—aka my blanket. I mostly stay in my room to catch up on Commander Bunny—my favorite streamer—videos. They're playing *BioBuild* again, and watching them makes me feel better because at least *someone* out there is still playing it, too.

One thing I did not take into account when planning for the field trip was how exhausting it would be to be around other people for four straight days. I see them at school, sure, but at least then I get to go home and socially unplug. Having to be School and Friend Maggie all day took more out of me than I thought.

But I'm awoken early Saturday morning—during *not* weekend hours—and I know my cocooning days are over.

Abuela technically may be an old lady (don't tell her I said that) but she always plays her music *so* loud on the weekends. Even louder than Dad, who still loves listening to screamo songs from when he was a teenager.

Abuela and her karaoke partner of a mop stop by my open bedroom door. "¡Levantate, niña!"

I refuse to get up and stay wrapped in my blanket. I am a caterpillar.

"¿Vas a dormir todo el día?"

I indignantly pop my head up. "All day? It's only seven in the morning! I haven't even slept in yet."

Abuela keeps singing to her outrageously loud song in Spanish as she and her mop dance down the hallway, calling over her shoulder, "¡El piso está mojado!"

I yank on a pair of socks and carefully follow the grout lines of our freshly mopped and still dangerously wet tile floor into the kitchen. "Why does she announce the floor is wet like some kind of threat?" I grumble.

Caro is wiping sleep from her eyes, her messy topknot a total bird's nest as she follows the same careful path ahead of me. The floor is lava game has nothing on an abuela with a mop.

Mom's in the kitchen drinking her tiny cup of Cuban coffee. She smiles when she sees us. "Look at my sleepy girls. Hurry up and get dressed."

"But it's Saturday," I whine. "And I don't have a track meet today."

"No, but it's prom," Mom says in a singsong voice with a smile.

Caro's eyes widen and she's fully awake in a snap. "It's *prom*!" she cries, and she sounds both excited and terrified. Her hands go to the top of her head and she screams. "My hair appointment is in like four hours!"

"Four hours, wow," I say, deadpan.

"I need to take a shower!" Caro spins around and runs back down the hall. A second later, there's a crashing sound and a yelp.

I shake my head with a tsk. "She forgot to stick to the grout lines."

A couple of hours later and I'm the one who's ready to scream. Mom promised fancy doughnuts if I came along, but I should have learned my lesson with the mall pretzel. Because every high school in Miami seems to also be having their prom today, which means the salon is super busy with shrieky teenagers.

I'm bored and hungry and Mom's pretty sick of my whining, so she distracts me with a manicure. At first, I don't want to bother with one, but  then I see the wall of pretty colors and cool designs.

While my fingernails are drying, my phone buzzes. It's a text from Zoey!

Zoey: Happy Saturday . . . I'm hanging out at Dolphin Park today, can't wait to hear everything 👀

Dolphin Park is right down the street. Mom takes pity on me when I beg her to let me go. Or maybe she's relieved to get me out of her hair, because she even buys Zoey and me lunch before dropping me off at the park.

"I'll be back as soon as your sister is done!" she calls out. That'll be a while since every teenager in Miami is getting a blowout in this humidity today.

I spot Zoey at a bench by the playground with a book. She jumps up and we run into a hug, squeezing the bag of French fries and nuggets. But I don't care. It's such a relief to finally see her after so long.

"Tell me everything!" Zoey says as she digs into the fries.

And I do! And she doesn't seem jealous or like she feels left out at all! She's smiling as she tells me about watching movies with her cousins and going fishing with her dad and actually sleeping without an alarm clock. She sounds so relaxed, and it unties the big stressful knot that was all tangled in my good feelings about the trip.

"Nice nails," Zoey says around a fry.

"Thanks." I admire them again. What's not to love about glittery stars?

"Are you going to get your hair done, too?" she teases.

I roll my eyes.

"Prom's a pretty big deal."

"I guess."

"And next week's the seventh-grade dance."

"Really?" we both ask each other at the same time.

With a shrug, Zoey admits, "Yeah. My mom said I can go, and I don't want to miss *another* thing." She no longer sounds super chill or relaxed. Maybe she does feel left out?

Worry starts to gnaw away at my earlier relief. I dust the salt and sand from my hands. "Well, I don't want to go with anyone."

Zoey eats another fry. "I don't think that's a requirement."

I look out at the ocean and think about Caro panicking this morning about her hair and don't envy her at all. I don't want all that stress and worry. But then I also think about her talking on the phone to Alex, laughing like she's having the best day ever, and how excited she was to find the perfect dress. I even overheard her saying they have a song now, and how cheesy is that? How embarrassing and ridiculous. I bet Eddie would never listen to a whiny soft song with sweet lyrics.

"Wait, you *do* want to go with someone," Zoey accuses me.

I snap out of my wandering thoughts. "I don't want to go with him!"

"Him who?"

Zoey asks so quickly—*too* quickly—that I immediately admit, "Eddie." My eyes widen. "Wait, no! That's not what I—"

And if that wasn't the worst thing ever, it's two voices who parrot back a surprised *"Eddie?"*

★ CHAPTER 20 ★

Seagulls loudly caw overhead, and I almost jump out of my skin again. This *has* to be a heart attack.

"Maggie, you are very red," Zoey says, then looks at Julian. "I didn't think she could blush."

Julian sets a hand on my forehead like he's checking if I have a fever. With a growl, I push his hand aside. "And what are you doing here?" I demand.

He shrugs. "It's Saturday."

It's such a simple answer, but it says so much. Because ever since I got my bike-riding privileges extended beyond school and the park, the three of us have hung out here after school and on Saturdays when we weren't busy with other stuff. But that was *before*. Before the field trip and Vanessa and . . . maybe Eddie? But definitely all these new feelings and stomachaches.

"I do *not* like Eddie." Why am I lying about this? I fully intended on confessing my crush to Zoey, but now my heart is racing and my face feels hot.

Zoey tips her head and studies me more closely. It reminds me of Mom. "I think you do . . ."

Julian cheers and shakes my shoulders and I feel like I'm made of a bunch of pieces that are now falling apart.

"He totally likes you, too," Julian tells me with so much confidence that my chest gets too tight to say anything. "Why didn't you tell me when I told you?"

Zoey looks at him. "Told her what?"

In my total and complete panic that Julian is about to break Zoey's heart, I flip to Latina Mom Mode™ to quickly put a stop to this.

LATINA MOM™

Crossed arms locked tight

Already doesn't believe you

Tapping foot

"No one has a crush!" I yell.

Zoey and Julian just look at me like I told them to go to their rooms.

"What did Julian tell you?" Zoey asks again, and this time she looks upset, like she is *definitely* feeling left out now. I can't keep this secret a second longer.

"Julian likes Vanessa!" I blurt.

Julian gasps. *"Maggie!"*

"What?" I shout. "This is all your fault!"

"How is this my fault!"

I scramble for an answer. "You never play *BioBuild* anymore—"

His mouth drops open. "My mom needs to renew my subscription!"

"And Zoey *likes* you likes you!"

"She . . . *what?*" Julian spins toward Zoey in a panic.

"No, I don't!" Zoey yelps.

I jump forward to reassure her. "It's okay! I was freaking out, too, when I realized, because what is this going to do to our friendship? What happens if he likes you back? I mean, of course he'll like you back, because you're amazing, but oh my gosh . . . what if you two start going out?" I start pacing in front of the bench as my thoughts fly out of me too quickly. "I didn't even think that far ahead. Will I be a third wheel? Will I have to stop hanging out with y'all so much? But wait . . . will you two hang out without me? But then what if you break up? Will I have to choose a side?"

"Maggie." Zoey holds me by the shoulders. "I do *not* like Julian. Like *that.*"

Julian stares off into the distance. "I'm so confused."

I start to reassure her that despite my squeaky, worried tone and how I'm sweating as badly as Julian whenever he has a secret, I'm actually very cool with all of this.

But looking her in the eye, I know she's being for real. She *doesn't* like Julian like that!

"Really? But all the signs . . . you were . . . I was so sure."

She shakes her head and sits down again. "I don't like anyone . . . like that." Zoey lets out a big gust of a sigh before saying, "Everyone is making such a big deal about all this dating and crush stuff. It's all anyone can talk about anymore. My band friends are all getting their hair straightened and acting like everything we do is to make somebody like us. *Everything* is about that now and it's been stressing me out. And then you two went on the field trip and had a bunch of fun without me. I was trying to be cool about it, but I just don't want to miss out on anything else. That's why I want to go to the dance."

"So, to recap." Julian points at me. "Maggie likes Eddie."

I cover my face with my hands and muffle a scream into them.

"Zoey likes no one," Julian goes on. "And I liked Vanessa . . . who actually likes Zoey."

Seventh grade is *so* confusing.

The last thing I want to deal with after all of these confusing revelations is Caro's prom chaos at home. So, after Mom picks me up, instead of going inside to face the circus of hairspray and glitter, I head over to Mrs. García's and quickly disappear within the wild, tropical garden.

I greet the chickens and roosters. I don't think too much about the source of the wind chimes and whether or not they're bones or driftwood, but instead enjoy their soft, tinkling music. And then I go check on my pumpkin seeds. I've been watering them weekly since we haven't gotten into our rainy season yet. And I'm happy to see that there are little green baby leaves and vines. I've never been prouder.

Except there's some-thing else growing here, too. Something different.

There are tall green stems. They better not be broccoli again! I had a whole plan!

Mrs. García is suddenly at my side, her unexpected appearance scaring me nearly out of my skin.

"Is that more broccoli?" I ask. "Because you told me they were pumpkin seeds!" Will none of my ideas go according to plan?

"Sí, *those* are pumpkins," she says, pointing at the collection of small sprouts defiantly poking up through the dirt. "Pero, esos son girasoles."

I study the other plants. Now that I look more closely at them, they do sort of look like flowers that haven't bloomed yet. What were sunflower seeds doing with my perfectly plotted out pumpkin seeds?

It's weird to think that these are all growing together but may not bloom at the same time. And when those pumpkins are big enough to carve? I'll be halfway into eighth grade! Who even knows what will be different by then? Will Zoey, Julian, and I still be the terrific trio? Will one of us . . . be in a couple?

Mrs. García waters the seeds. "Learning when it's time to let go of your plans is learning the difference between all of your worries and what you know to be true."

I shake my head. "That makes no sense."

She smiles in her sneaky bruja way. "As you move forward through uncertainty, it will."

Caro, Alex, and their friends make silly faces for the camera. If I'm feeling a *tiny* bit jealous, it's only because they're having a great time, while it feels like my friend group is in shambles.

Julian isn't online playing *BioBuild*. No one is texting in the group chat after our weird afternoon at the park. It *was* a lot of information and emotion to digest.

So, while my sister is at away at her magical prom, I decide to hang out with Abuela and Mrs. García and the rest of their new bowling league. It gets me out of the house and distracts me from feeling lonely even though I *am* losing to a bunch of old people. But at least there's nachos and extra tokens for the arcade.

But the next day, I can't help but be curious. Because Caro is *glowing*. Her hair looks exactly like it did when she walked out of the salon and when she and Alex get back from brunch, they bring me a milk tea and show us all their pictures. They look right out of a movie.

Dad reminisces about his prom. Abuela proclaims them both beautiful. Mom's practically swooning over every

picture with total hearts in her eyes. And I can't help but secretly imagine my friends and me in those—glittery, fun, and maybe a little dreamy—pictures.

It probably wasn't *really* like that, though. I bet it's just their camera filters.

★ CHAPTER 21 ★

At school on Monday, there are posters *everywhere* about the upcoming seventh-grade dance. They're around every corner and even follow me down the halls between classes.

With spring break behind us, my entire class is all dance, all the time now. Everyone is talking about their dresses and dates. My friends, though? They're a mess. As soon as I reach our lunch table, Julian pounces on me. He's looking stressed. Like he-just-walked-219-steps-to-the-top-of-the-lighthouse stressed.

"I think I messed up," he tells me with a wide-eyed look.

"What did you do now?"

"I told Zoey that Vanessa likes her! I shouldn't have done that. My loyalties got all crisscrossed. Zoey is my best friend, but Vanessa is also my friend now."

I peel open my applesauce. "Being caught in the middle isn't easy."

"Yeah, but—"

Vanessa sits down and Julian's mouth shuts closed on whatever else he was about to say.

"Hey, roommate!" Vanessa says to me with a big smile, then quickly glances around. "Where's Zoey?"

Zoey stopped a couple of tables over to chat with Maya and some of her band friends as usual. Julian is looking at me like someone who just robbed a bank and now *really* needs to tell someone where they stashed the diamonds.

"What's wrong?" Vanessa asks him.

Julian is turning red as a tomato. He's also sweating a lot. He always sweats when he has a secret, but even for

him, this is a lot. He looks like he does in PE after running the mile. When Zoey sits down across from him, his eyes bug out. If I took a picture of him right now, it would definitely become a meme.

Panic!

I really hope he's wearing deodorant.

"Hey, Zoey," Vanessa says.

"Hi!" Zoey chirps brightly. Her eyes nervously dart between Vanessa and Julian.

The drama of this situation is worse than one of Abuela's telenovelas.

Vanessa is smart and puts two and two together pretty quickly. And between Julian's sweaty outburst and Zoey's big, bright, but immovable smile, I'm pretty sure it would be obvious even to me if I hadn't already known. Probably.

Vanessa jumps out of her seat with a mumbled excuse about going to the bathroom.

All this tension is driving a wedge between my friends and I'm tired of it. We need to face this head-on. Get it over with. Look at Caro and all her friends! If they can have it all figured out, then so can we. I can be brave like Pablo. As fun as Alex. And I'm *definitely* cooler than Caro. This will be like ripping off a Band-Aid. Like unexpected sunflowers when you thought you only planted pumpkins. I push my tray away and get to my feet. I march past the other tables to sit down next to Eddie.

"Hey," he says.

"Hey," I say, too loudly, and clear my throat. "So, I was wondering . . ." I start to hesitate, but remind myself that communication is key. Confidence, too. I got this. "Do you want to go to the dance?"

There! I did it! Now Julian and Vanessa and Zoey will figure it out, too. This isn't that big of a deal.

Eddie's brows pull together in a confused frown. "What?"

"With me?" I tack on just as he says, "No," in a quiet but horrified tone.

We stare at each other for three torturous seconds before I say, "Cool." I get to my feet  and march away like a robot. My heart is beating like a drum and it's all I can hear in my ears. Better that than the laughing I'm sure is following in my wake. I walk right past my lunch table, where a wide-eyed Zoey and Julian are watching me. But I can't stop. I go all the way to the bathroom and find Vanessa standing in front of the mirror.

As soon as the door closes behind me, Vanessa asks, "Did Julian tell Zoey I like her?"

"Yes," I admit, because I don't want to lie to her. She's our friend, too. And because she's my friend, I ask her, in a strangled voice, "Do you have a pad?"

Her eyes widen, but she nods quickly and digs inside her bag. She hands me a small square and I duck into a stall. I'm not on my period. I haven't even gotten mine yet. But I'm about to lie and pretend I have and that I need to go home right this second, because there's no way I'm *ever* going back out there.

When Mom picks me up from the nurse's office, she reassures me everything's going to be okay in her soft, soothing voice. It's the one she uses when she doesn't want me to panic. When we get to the car, before I even have a chance to tell her that I haven't actually started my period yet—she shows me The Kit.

It's like a first-aid kit meets the hurricane kit she keeps in case of any storms. This one used to be filled with toys,

snacks, and other bright, distracting kid stuff to entertain us when Caro and I were younger, but it now includes deodorant, a hairbrush, phone chargers, and, yes, menstrual products.

"Mom," I say, stopping her before she grabs anything for me. "I didn't start yet. I just . . . panicked."

"Oh . . . okay." Mom deflates a little in the driver's seat. With relief? I can't tell. For a split second, she looks like she's going to switch to rapid-fire Spanish and complain about having to leave work early to pick me up for nothing, because don't I know how busy she is during the day? But after another look at me, she softens instead.

"Did you get a chance to eat lunch?" she asks.

At the mention of lunch, I sink deeper into the passenger seat. I'm going to have to give up my table outside and start eating in the cafeteria instead.

"How about a batido de mango?"

At the mention of my favorite milkshake, I sit up at once. A mango milkshake won't save this disaster of a day, but it can't make it worse.

*   *   *

Abuela is surprised to see me home early, but thankfully, Mom keeps it simple and only mentions that I'm not feeling well. Abuela, being Abuela, goes into full detective mode and insists on taking my temperature. Then she makes me put on a beanie hat she recently made with her knitting club and some thick socks or else that lethal chilly air might be the death of me.

My abuela is on a lifelong mission to make sure I'm never barefoot.

I don't complain and try to look as pathetic as possible because there's no way I can go back to school tomorrow. Maybe Mom can sign me up for virtual or homeschooling. It might be tough with the school year almost over, but I can go back for eighth grade after everyone forgets this humiliating catastrophe over the summer. That's what I need—a good old-fashioned summer shuffle of new haircuts and growth spurts. By then no one will remember whatever Eddie is telling them right now.

There's a tiny part of me that doesn't believe Eddie would make fun of me—or anyone, really—but I still

remember overhearing Slimy Steven laughing it up with the rest of the Chads after school when Chloe Williams asked him to be her boyfriend. It was not very nice.

Luckily caterpillars like me have no use for crushes or butterflies.

★ CHAPTER 22 ★

Mom disagrees with my caterpillar status the next morning.

She won't even stop to consider my plans to be home-schooled starting immediately. Even after I promise to make a very effective PowerPoint about all the benefits to us working and doing school from home. We'll get to hang out all the time! Think of all the mango milkshakes! The arts and crafts! We can knit with Abuela!

Needless to say, she does not think of the mango milkshakes or knitting possibilities. And then Caro unhelpfully reminds me that I have track practice today. I have to go to school, which means I'm left with only one option: a disguise.

"You can't wear a hat to school," Mom insists. She's no longer using her soft and soothing voice. This is her hurry-up-or-you're-going-to-make-me-late voice. "And it's too hot for that jacket."

I take off the hat but remind her that I am a Florida tween. I survive August in Miami while wearing a black sweater and eating Takis.

I ride my bike super slow to school and arrive just before the bell. Down every hallway, I keep my guard up, waiting to overhear someone whispering about me to their friends.

All clear so far. No one says anything in homeroom, but in social studies, someone laughs, and my shoulders hunch up to my ears in an effort to disappear. But it's just Alicia showing Dominique a funny meme on her phone.

The real test is after PE, because I have science with Eddie.

But he's mysteriously absent. I'm starting to relax until the bell for lunch.

Mom won't let me be a caterpillar, and now my friends won't let me become a tree. The lack of support is a real mood killer. Just to be extra sure he's really absent, I quickly check Eddie's usual spot on my way to my seat. He isn't here, either. My stomach is still in weird knots, but I'm relieved. I think. Or maybe I'm even more anxious? It's honestly hard to tell.

"I really thought he liked you back," Julian says, confused.

"Don't start."

Zoey leans close and whispers, "It was very brave of you to ask him."

The sincerity in her voice gets me. "And look how that turned out. I was just trying to put a stop to all the weirdness between us and now everyone is having a big laugh about me."

But neither Zoey nor Julian has heard a thing about it. I'm not the hot topic, punch line, or main character of the day. And as we study all the other tables around us, it's clear that no one is laughing at me or even looking our way.

"Where's Vanessa?" I ask.

Julian's face falls. "She's been avoiding me."

"And now me, too," Zoey says with a sigh.

It's just the three of us again. No intruders or new friends. No crushes or confusion. The terrific trio. It's exactly how I wanted it.

Right?

I have practice after school. Down on the track, I spot Caro setting out cones. "This is for you to work on your high jump."

My nemesis. The jump, not Caro. Well, not totally Caro. She is still *not* my coach, but she is very stubborn. I've been struggling with the high jump all season and have yet to make it on a first try.

After I warm up, Coach Schwartz leaves me to Caro. I run through the drills along the cones she set out to work on my jump. She's patient as she watches me run those ten steps over and over. She moves the cones according to whatever mental math she's doing.

Caro finally decides I'm ready. We head over to the high jump.

"Start here." She points at a spot on the track. "And run it just like you've been doing all afternoon."

I face down the high jump. It's not that high. Not like you see on the Olympics or anything, but for whatever reason, it's gotten me every time. It's frustrating not being good at something I want to be good at. And I really want something to go right.

I take three slow, steadying breaths. And then I run.

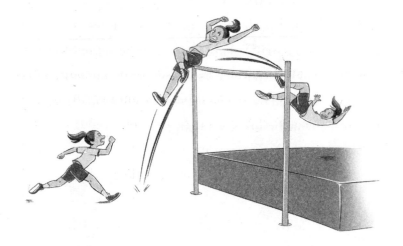

I did it!

"Yay, Maggie!"

It's Sammy, Alicia, and Mia from the other side of the track. Even Coach whistles for me. My heart is pounding but I feel like I'm floating. I'm so excited that I jump over to Caro and hug her.

"I am an awesome coach," she says with a laugh, and I push her away, also laughing.

I turn around to do it again. Just before I do, I glance up at the stands and spot Eddie. I freeze.

He waves at me. I think. His hand falls down too quickly for me to tell or even respond before Sammy, Alicia, and Mia run over and throw their arms around me, screaming about the high jump in my ear. By the time I get out of their huddle, I see Eddie hurrying down the stairs. I think he might be headed toward the track but instead I watch him leave, skating off through the mostly empty parking lot and then out to the sidewalk.

What in the world was that about?

Despite all the buzz over this Saturday's dance, there's not one single whisper about me totally failing with Eddie. From anyone. It's almost like it didn't even happen, and I feel weirdly comforted by the show of loyalty. Or maybe it just wasn't that big of a deal to him. The only strange blip is him being at my practice, but maybe that was a coincidence? Maybe Eddie is a secret rule breaker and likes to skate at the track after school once everyone's gone but didn't know we would be there.

I have a meet on Saturday, which would normally distract me from thinking about the dance, except it's all any of the other seventh graders are talking about. When I land my high jump on the first try, Sammy congratulates me again. And then immediately asks me if I'm going to the dance.

"No," I tell her, still a little breathless after my jump.

"Why not?"

"Because I'm super busy today and have other stuff to do."

When we stop at the supermarket, I'm excited to see Pablo. Maybe I don't have a busy calendar or dance to

look forward to, but I do have whatever fancy dessert he's making today.

I take a huge bite and then let my head fall onto the counter. My hand flies up to give him a thumbs-up and he laughs.

"Guess what?" he asks.

I sit up and take a sip of my pineapple soda. "What?"

"I got a job at that new restaurant!"

"That's awesome, Pablo!"

"My parents are being surprisingly supportive about it. You were right about making a plan and sticking to it," he tells me. "Because

sometimes you really just have to go for it."

My smile disappears. "You have to be careful, though. Because sometimes you go for stuff and then it blows up in your face."

"Uh-oh, what happened?"

There's no way I'm going to tell Pablo. Sure, he's been a good friend and has listened to me complain about stuff before, but he's basically an adult. Not nearly as old as the viejitos who hang around the window and bakery to trade gossip over their Cuban coffees, but still.

"If you need someone to listen . . ."

"Okay, okay," I say, and take back the offered plate. "I asked a boy to the  school dance and he said no."

"Oh noooo." Pablo holds a hand over his heart and shakes his head slowly. "Been there."

"Yeah, I didn't even know I liked him and then it was like whoa. I *do* like him. He's this like total e-boy—" I glance up at Pablo's new green hair and eyeliner. "Which is cool, of course.

Go on . . .

"And he's nice and funny and has way too many earrings on one ear compared to the other, but whatever. At least he didn't tell everyone about my total fail."

Pablo seems thoughtful all of a sudden. And then he smiles like he just realized something. "Miami can be such a small town sometimes."

I wolf down the apple tart. "I guess," I say around my last bite.

"And if you really want to go to that dance . . . I say go for it. We only get so many dances in life, you know?"

I'm about to tell him no way, but the thing is . . . I *do* want to go to the dance. Just like I wanted to go to the field trip and on ghost tours and to the park by the beach with my friends. I want silly group pictures and to wear that dress that matches the glittery stars that are still on my nails. I want to dance to cheesy pop songs.

I'm going to the dance . . . and this time I know just who to ask.

★ CHAPTER 23 ★

Tonight it's my turn to have my whole family take a hundred pictures of me standing awkwardly next to the palm tree in our front yard in a dress.

"Our neighbors are looking at us." I wave at Mrs. García, who's sitting on her front porch with a cat *and* a rooster.

"Because you look amazing!" Dad says as he snaps photos on his phone.

Abuela whistles for my attention, then directs me how to pose. She pushes her hip out. Gross.

"Smile with your whole face!" Caro calls out for the third time. I still don't know what that means.

Lucas sits at Mom's feet but takes off in his speed crawl toward me. He's not walking yet, but he's definitely getting close. His first birthday party is later this month. My parents are making a *huge* deal out of it and inviting the whole neighborhood. Dad's even going to roast a pig. In our backyard. Yes, you heard me right. My father is going to roast a pig in the pit he dug in our backyard. It's a very Cuban thing to do.

"All right, paparazzi, show's over," I call out, and hand Lucas to Mom. I check that he didn't get any dirt on my dress.

Dad spins the car keys on his finger. "Time to take my baby girl to her first dance." His smile slips as his bottom lip quivers.

Mom sighs. "Here we go."

"Ay dios," Abuela mumbles.

Caro shakes her head. "He did this last week, too."

"Come on, Dad," I say, and pull him toward the car. "I'll even let you pick the music."

His face lights up. "I know just the playlist!" Dad bumps my fist. Mom confirms what time the dance ends, so she knows when to pick me up.

"Ooh, out after nine," Caro says. "Big night."

I wave goodbye to Mrs. García and she calls out a reminder about the full moon tonight and to be careful. Definitely a bruja.

Dad drops me off in front of the school. It's a short drive so he's only on the second song of his playlist. As soon as I open the door, the clamorous sounds of a guy singing about some place on Ocean Avenue spill out. Several teachers and chaperones glance over at us. Not to reprimand, but to sing along to Dad's total delight.

"What . . . is . . . happening?" I slowly mutter under my breath. Dad raises the volume. I screech and duck away before the chorus. Outside the gym, I spot my friend waiting for me.

"Vanessa!"

Her brown dress has thin straps and she's wearing a white T-shirt underneath. She's also got on very cool boots.

"I'm so glad you came," I tell her. "We've missed you at lunch this week."

She blushes. "Are you sure you all weren't talking about me? Again?"

It lands like a punch. But I'm ready, because she's right. "Julian shouldn't have said anything. You're his friend just like Zoey is. But I have found this to be a confusing year and crushes have made it more complicated." I try for a smile and shrug. "But we're all still figuring it out."

Vanessa smiles back. But it falls when we spot Julian and Zoey across the courtyard. Zoey looks amazing in a yellow dress that flares out at her knees, and Julian is not only wearing pants instead of shorts for the first time that I've ever seen, but he's got on a button-up shirt *and* tie.

"I just don't want any weirdness," Vanessa quietly admits.

"I can't promise that," I tell her. "It's been a *very* weird year. But you're one of us now and I *can* promise we'll be there for one another."

Julian shuffles his feet when he reaches us. "Hey." He sounds like a kicked puppy.

Vanessa smirks as she playfully shoves his shoulder. "So. You *can't* keep a secret."

"I'm so sorry!" he wails.

"He sweats uncontrollably whenever he has one," Zoey says.

"Hey, look at us," I say.

"Who would have thought?" Julian asks.

"Not me!" Zoey finishes with a laugh.

We head inside, where it's even noisier than Dad's car. The gym vibrates with a booming song, and it doesn't look at all in here like it does during PE. The overhead lights are low and there's a DJ set up in the corner. Some of our classmates are already dancing.

"Our first dance." I try not to sound as nervous as I feel, but sweat prickles the back of my neck and under my arms. "What should we do first?"

"Dance," Zoey says, then hesitates when the song gets faster. "No, we should eat first. Is that pizza? But I'm not hungry. Maybe I'm thirsty. Oh no . . . am I dehydrated?"

Vanessa offers, "Let's walk the room once so that we can see everything and then we'll decide."

"Good idea," Zoey and I say at the same time.

Our first official school dance and the fearsome foursome are a mess.

Until we're saved by the new girl who's not so new anymore. Who's actually pretty amazing.

Vanessa asks, "Do you want to dance?"

"Me?" Julian and Zoey ask at the same time.

Vanessa laughs with a bright smile. "All of us . . . as a group." She motions toward the dance floor, where a lot more people are dancing now. I'm not the best dancer in the world, but I know the next song! It's that DJ Junior Peña one that was super popular at the beginning of the year. Julian, Zoey, Vanessa, and I all rush out to middle of the dance floor.

Thanks to Vanessa's confidence, we finally relax. We dance and laugh and take goofy pictures and dare one another to request songs from the DJ. Teachers dance to the throwback songs and we laugh more. It's that glittery, fun, and a little bit dreamy feeling I felt while looking at Caro's pictures of her prom. And while Julian might like Vanessa who maybe likes Zoey and I asked a boy to a dance who said—

My first instinct is to run to the bathroom and hide again. But then Eddie sees me and starts walking toward me.

Do you want to dance?

"What did you do, Julian?" I hiss under my breath.

"Nothing!" he says, then smirks. "I told you I was right."

My heart has somehow ping-ponged out of my chest and flown up into my throat, where it is now officially stuck. I still somehow manage a silent nod.

The faster song slows down into one of those whiny soft songs with sweet lyrics that Caro listens to on repeat. I'm sweating again. Who starts the dance?

We sway in place. Are we on beat? My brain can hardly keep up. I'm dancing with the boy I asked to the dance. The one who said no. But now he's here and I just *really* hope I don't smell like pepperoni pizza.

"I was surprised when you asked me," he says.

I can't look him in the face, so I focus on a lime-green streamer in the corner. "Oh. Sorry about that."

"No, I just . . . I didn't plan on coming to this," he continues quietly. "Not really my scene."

We sway some more. I try not to step on him.

"So . . . why are you here, then?" I ask, confused by the conversation.

He shrugs and I figure that's his answer until he says, "Because you asked me."

"And my brother told me you were going to be here tonight."

"Really?" I say, surprised. "Who's your brother?" How did he know?

Miami really can be a small town sometimes.

⋆ CHAPTER 24 ⋆

It is official. I, Maggie Diaz, have a boyfriend!

Just kidding! I only *just* got my Cuban American parents to let me have a phone! Can you even imagine how long until they let me *date*? It's cool, because I'm not ready for all the  drama. A crush, though? That I can handle. A crush who shows up at a dance for me?

Hello, core memory.

Eddie's a better friend now who texts me sometimes and makes my stomach flip-flop a lot. Someone who I maybe think about when I listen to soft, whiny songs with sweet lyrics. But unlike my sister—and dad—I do not blast those songs at full volume for the whole neighborhood to hear.

Oh, and did I mention that Eddie plays *BioBuild*?

But today isn't about me (hey, even I can share the spotlight) because today is about my baby brother and the whole neighborhood coming over to celebrate his birthday.

Dad's been up since five in the morning monitoring the roast pork like any slight change in the wind might affect the outcome. A bunch of the old men of the neighborhood who Abuela roped into joining her bowling team have come over and they're all giving Dad advice (and critiques) he didn't ask for. Kind of like Caro always trying to coach me when it comes to running.

Mom told me that Caro is just super stressed about getting everything done for her college applications and this is her way of showing me attention. But my sister is obnoxiously good at everything and will get into any school she wants. She's what some might call brilliant and always achieves whatever she sets her mind to.

I would never say that to her face, though.

But if Caro does decide to go away to college, she only has a year left of living at home with us. It's weird to think about that. The other night I looked up all the colleges listed on the

whiteboard in her room. And then I measured the distance between them and home.

I only did that because I was curious. Not because I'll miss her or anything. It'll be great to not fight her every morning because she hogs the bathroom to do her hair, leaving strands of it everywhere. And I'll no longer have to listen to songs blasting from her room while I'm trying to do homework. And she won't be around to quiz me about my race times. And since she won't be able to take *all* her clothes with her when she moves out, she won't know if I borrow a shirt she leaves behind.

Unlike today, when she definitely noticed.

"Why are you trying to look nice?" she asks with a suspicious sneer.

"It's a birthday party."

"No, that's not it." She studies me. "You're trying to look cute for some reason. I'm humbled you decided to raid my closet to achieve that."

"Humble is not a word I would use to describe you."

"Give me back my shirt," she demands, but I'm saved by Alex's arrival.

Caro switches to cool girlfriend mode whenever Alex is around. She doesn't want to sink to bickering with her little sister in front of her. But we're sisters who have been arguing since the moment Mom and Dad brought me home, so we're both fluent in a very specific shared sisterly language. Which means I understand that her angry gaze is threatening me bodily harm if I get anything on her shirt.

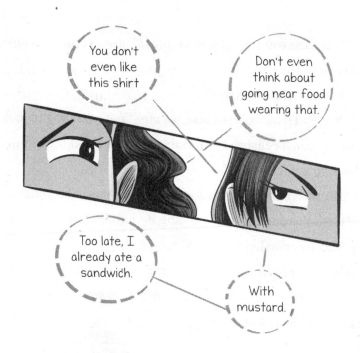

Caro shrieks and chases me, but I dash away with a laugh. She must really love this shirt.

We circle the yard and giant inflatable bounce house but then crash to a sudden stop at Mom's shout.

"Everyone look!" she calls out. "Lucas is walking!

"I've got one kid just learning to walk and another almost to college." Mom shakes her head with a laugh. "And here I thought I was good at math."

An old salsa song about laughing and crying starts to play from the speakers. Abuela picks up a laughing Lucas and spins him right into an energetic dance. Mom pulls Dad away from his grill long enough to dance. And before I know it, everyone is dancing to the song, even Caro and me with my clumsy moves. Sibling secret languages and fights aside, it will be really sad to not have her right down the hall.

Because maybe I will miss her. A lot. But don't tell her that.

The party is in full swing when I spot some very familiar faces.

"I could smell the food from several blocks away," Julian says with a look that's halfway to drooling.

Zoey hands me a gift bag. "Some cat ears for your brother. I stole them from my sister."

I laugh. "Nice!"

"Thanks for inviting me," Vanessa says.

"Of course!" I point my thumb toward the bounce house behind me. "Who's ready to get in there?"

I love my friends because they all immediately shout, *"Me!"* before racing to the huge monstrosity currently taking up half my backyard. Just because we're seventh graders doesn't mean we have to hurry up and become boring or too grown-up to do something as fun as jump in a bounce house. We're not too old to play the same video games we've loved since elementary school. It's nice to realize we don't have to rush past this part.

I leap right into the fray.

"Maggie!" Mom calls just as I'm about to attempt a double bounce. I pop my head out of the netting to look for Mom, who is standing with a few others, pointing toward me. I almost fall forward at the sight of who she's with.

I smile and wave. Behind me, my friends lean their heads out, too.

"Edgy Eddie," Julian whispers right next to me.

"Enamored Eddie," Zoey says.

"Exciting Eddie," Vanessa adds, in on the nickname jokes now.

"*Hey*, Eddie!" I loudly call out, then whisper a mumbled threat over my shoulder about unplugging the bounce house's blowers. "And Pablo and Ms. Lopez!" I tack on quickly.

Eddie says something to my mom that makes her smile before he hands her the gift. It's springtime in Miami, so it's already super hot outside, but Eddie looks cool and collected in a black sweater and dark jeans that have a chain across the pocket. By the look of Mom's narrow-eyed concentration, I'm pretty sure she's counting his earrings.

This is my first time having a boy over who isn't Julian and it feels significant.

"¡Hola, Eddie!" Abuela calls with a big smile.

Abuela might have thought Eddie was spooky on the

field trip, but now they're buddied up and are making a beeline toward Dad and all the food. I practically tumble out of the bounce house in my rush to get to them before Dad can ask him if he's boiling beneath that sweater.

"Hey, Eddie, how can you tell that a burger was grilled in space?" Dad is asking him when I reach them.

Oh no.

"It's a little . . . meteor."

Dad laughs. Eddie smiles. I die only a little. And then Dad spots the wallet chain and starts to tell Eddie about some concert he went to in the *nineties*.

"You sure that isn't burning, Dad?"

"What?" Dad spins back to the grill and I hurry Eddie away.

He follows me with his hands in his pockets, and between the casual stroll, vintage wallet chain, and my flip-flopping stomach, I'm starting to worry that inviting him over to my baby brother's birthday party was the wrong idea. Not because I don't want him here, because I do. But maybe despite him still playing *BioBuild* and being cool enough to hug my abuela without getting embarrassed, he'll think it's silly or immature to jump in a bounce house. And that would be a huge disappointment, because crush or not, I don't want to be boring and beyond bounce houses.

But before I can say a word, Eddie slips his shoes off and climbs right inside.

The school year is almost over, which means we have a whole summer ahead of us where everything will change *again*. Clubs, crushes, friends. Sisters applying to college, brothers learning to talk, me headed to my last year of middle school. Caterpillars becoming butterflies. It turns out that the rest of seventh grade wasn't a total piece of cake like I planned. But there's definitely a slice of Pablo's *amazing* cake in our immediate future. Because life is unexpected and awesome and sometimes nothing goes according to my plans.

And isn't that the best?

Acknowledgments

I love all of my books. There are no favorite children here. Trust me, as a middle child, I'd know. But something about this one felt . . . perfect. This is my first time writing a sequel, and when all was said and mostly edited, this book—initially and lovingly titled 2 Maggie 2 Diaz— became the exact story I'd hoped to tell. The one I wish I could have found at a school book fair when I was an anxious, hopeful, always daydreaming seventh grader. And I have to say, it's tough for *anything* about seventh grade to feel that way.

Maggie Diaz would not be Maggie Diaz without Courtney Lovett's incredible art. Being a writer means being stuck in my head most days, but luckily enough, Courtney will take an idea and create magic. From that bright cover to that classroom page the deserves to be a poster, I'm eternally grateful to get to work on this story with you. Thank you for loving these characters (and their hair) as much as I do. And thank you to Asia Simone for your incredible illustrations! You brought so much love to Maggie and company! Thank you to Shelly Romero for asking me to do this again and for championing our chaotic child every step of the way. Para siempre, mi amor. To Talia Seidenfeld for being my surprise bus buddy who helped me find my way to butterflies. And to Tiffany Colón for jumping right into Team Maggie with so much excitement, love, and your own Abuela stories. Thank you to Maeve Norton for designing the book of my dreams *again*. I'll be forever grateful to you for that pink bus and gorgeous coral pink cover. From clubs to crushes and weird Florida field trips, thank you to Melissa Schirmer, Lizette Serrano, Victoria Velez, and everyone at Scholastic for loving and supporting our stubbornly optimistic planner.

To my agent, Laura Crockett. Middle grade, who would have thought? Thank you for being *my* stubbornly optimistic planner who always has my back. Teamwork makes the dream work, and there's no better team than Triada.

To my family for their loyalty, pride, and like, decades worth of inside jokes. I'm the one gasping for air as I crack myself up halfway through a story, but y'all still always laugh anyway. I sneak little nods to each of you in my books . . . but you'll have to buy them to find them. Y a mi abuelo. Siempre estuviste tan orgulloso de mí. Tu gorda linda te extraña tanto.

Thank you to all of my writer and reader friends who always offer so much support and camaraderie, even as

I jump between middle and high school. I'm so lucky to have you in my life, inbox, and on my shelves. Shout-out to Tehlor Kay Mejia and Avery for being one of the first to read and root for Maggie!

And to every single teacher, librarian, and bookseller who places books into readers' hands. I'm here because of your unique, life-affirming, eternal magic. Thank you, thank you, *thank you*.

About the Author

Nina Moreno was born and raised in Miami until a hurricane sent her family toward the pines of Georgia. Her young adult novel, *Don't Date Rosa Santos*, was a Junior Library Guild Selection, Indie Next Pick for teen readers, and SIBA Okra Pick. You can find her online at ninamoreno.com.

About the Illustrators

Courtney Lovett received her BFA in Visual Arts and Animation from the University of Maryland, Baltimore County. She works in different mediums and artistic disciplines, including illustration, character design, and animation. As a Black American and a native of the DC, Maryland, Virginia area, her work reflects her heritage and upbringing, which adds to today's cultural shift of creating diverse and relatable stories from perspectives that are often underrepresented or misrepresented in art and media. You can find her online at courtneylovett.com.

Asia Simone received her BFA in Illustration and minor in creative writing from the University of the Arts. She is a Philly native artist with artistic disciplines in illustration and animation. She also writes stories that speak to her unique perspective of growing up as a young Black girl in America with a love for media that she did not often see herself in. She uses vibrant colors, shapes, and light to express fantasy in reality and to showcase positive representations of underrepresented people and stories. You can find her at asiaillustration.com.